37 THINGS
I LOVE

IN NO PARTICULAR ORDER

KEKLA MAGOON

Kekla Magoon (signature)

37 THINGS I LOVE

IN NO PARTICULAR ORDER

SQUARE
FISH

HENRY HOLT AND COMPANY

NEW YORK

SQUARE FISH

An Imprint of Macmillan
175 Fifth Avenue
New York, NY 10010
mackids.com

Square Fish and the Square Fish logo are trademarks of Macmillan and
are used by Henry Holt and Company under license from Macmillan.

Square Fish books may be purchased for business or promotional use.
For information on bulk purchases, please contact the Macmillan
Corporate and Premium Sales Department at
(800) 221-7945 x 5442 or by e-mail at specialmarkets@macmillan.com.

Library of Congress Cataloging-in-Publication Data
Magoon, Kekla.
37 things I love (in no particular order) / Kekla Magoon.
p.   cm.
Summary: Fifteen-year-old Ellis recalls her favorite things as her
mother's desire to turn off the machines that have kept Ellis's father alive
for two years fill the last four days of her sophomore year with major
changes in herself and her relationships.
ISBN 978-1-250-03430-4 (paperback) / ISBN 978-1-4299-4170-9 (e-book)
[1. Self-actualization (Psychology)—Fiction.   2. Interpersonal relations—
Fiction.   3. Coma—Fiction.   4. Grief—Fiction.   5. High schools—
Fiction.   6. Schools—Fiction.]   I. Title.   II. Title: Thirty-seven
things I love (in no particular order).
PZ7.M2739Aam 2012   [Fic]—dc23   2011031998

Originally published in the United States by Henry Holt and Company
First Square Fish Edition: 2013
Book designed by April Ward
Square Fish logo designed by Filomena Tuosto

10   9   8   7   6   5   4   3   2   1

AR: 3.7 / LEXILE: HL600L

For my mom

37 THINGS
I LOVE

IN NO PARTICULAR ORDER

1

Wings

If humans had them, the world might just be perfect.

I LOOK FOR WAYS to stop myself from falling. The air is wide beneath me. Wide and warm. The beam, cold and narrow. This balancing act will end with me spread wingless in the sky, no idea how it happened—maybe I closed my eyes at the very wrong moment. Then I'm tumbling, tearing, down, down . . .

The scream that rips out of me is so familiar, I recognize its taste before I even hear the sound. My stomach soars into my throat, about to choke me, when I buck and come awake.

The dream. It's only the dream. I clutch the edge of my mattress, which is on the floor. There's nowhere to fall from here, but I feel as if I'm groping the air.

Mom appears in the doorway. She crosses the

room with fleet footsteps and puts the washcloth in my hand, cool and soothing. I press it to my face as she settles down beside me.

This is our routine.

Mom scoops the hair away from my cheeks. Her hands are small and swift. She says nothing. She's tried every comfort word already and learned that saying nothing is always safest.

I get that she doesn't know what to do with the dream, or with me. The inside of her slim wrist strokes my cheek, maybe by accident.

It's almost time to get up. Light seeps in under the curtains, and Mom's here, still dressed in her work clothes.

Her fingers sweep through my hair, every strand, repairing the loose ponytail I was sleeping in. By the time she's finished, my grip on the mattress has relaxed. I hold on to her arm, knowing she has both feet on the ground.

I don't like the worried look on her face, or the urgent way she strokes my hand, trying to calm me down.

When I lie back against the pillows, she stops and holds my hands between hers.

"I'M HAVING FETTUCCINE," Mom says, pressing buttons on the coffeemaker. "What do you want for breakfast?"

It's things like this that make me sure that we will never talk about the dream. Never talk about anything that matters.

"Oatmeal, I think."

"Raisins?"

"Yeah."

Mom stretches high to reach the Quaker Oats carton. It's only the second-highest shelf, but she wobbles on tiptoe, like a beginner ballerina. At times it's hard to believe we're even related. Mom is thin. Rail thin. Dirty-looks-from-passersby thin. Eating-disorder-ad thin, but just by nature. She loses weight when she sneezes. Sometimes I think she loses weight when *I* sneeze.

Her voice doesn't match her body. Not at all. People never guess she's Laura Baldwin, late-night radio goddess, by looking at her. Mom has this deep-throated voice like hot milk on chocolate. Her voice is her job, her life. Her voice is this amazing gift to the world.

To look or sound like her, all small and throaty, is a different kind of dream. Standing side by side, we seem like strangers.

I head for the coffeepot as Mom shifts to the stove. She starts heating water for my oatmeal. Then she nukes the leftover fettuccine from my dinner last night for herself.

Mom works nights at the radio station, so she cooks me dinner while she cooks herself breakfast, and vice versa. We hardly ever eat the same thing at the same time. According to my guidance counselors, this makes me more likely to be "troubled."

But it works for us. Mom sleeps during the day while I'm at school, so she'll be awake when I get home. If I come home late, she knows I've been to see Dad. Those are the days when she bakes cookies. It's funny, because Mom's not at all domestic like that.

She leaves for work at the radio station late at night. Her on-air shift is midnight to four A.M., and she's always home by six, when I'm getting up for school.

It's five thirty now. In two hours, I'll have to leave for school. Four days until summer vacation, and I'm counting the minutes.

"We need to talk," Mom says, over fettuccine and oatmeal.

"Huh?" My spoon slips, clattering against the bowl.

Mom and I do great at not talking. It's not a hostile thing. There just aren't any words lost between us. Mom saves up her thoughts for when she's on air.

I don't have a whole lot to say. At least not to her.

"I want us to talk," Mom says. "About your father."

I push my bowl away half full.

She's dragging me across the invisible line, straight into the never-ever domain. I am shaken.

"Ellis, I think it's time."

She couldn't be more wrong.

2
Dad

My hero. In all ways but one, perfect.

I STAND OUTSIDE the building I call ALF, lingering on a path that I'm usually happy to follow. I rarely come here before school, but this is an emergency.

I pace in the grass. In two years, I've never hesitated for a second on the way to visit Dad. Today, I don't know what I'm going to say.

It shouldn't be this hard.

Dad knows everything about me. Every wound and how I got it. Every scar, the ones you can see and the ones you can't.

I tell him things I didn't even know it was possible to say out loud, until I say them and they're out there, in the air. He listens, never judges me. Never says anything that would make me feel bad.

Or good.

Taking a deep breath, I glide in through the main doors of the nursing home, the Assisted Living Facility, aka ALF.

I push open the door to his room. "Hi, Dad."

The machine beside his bed hisses, this eternal sound. That's how he sounds to me now. The voice that I will always remember as his.

I go to the side of his bed and take his hand. I know he's glad to see me. I'm sure he knows I'm here.

When he goes, it'll be me and Mom. Mostly, it will be me alone.

I WAS THIRTEEN, but I barely remember the construction accident two years ago. Some flashes, but that's it. All I know is, Dad was here one day and not here the next.

Dad owns a construction company; that day he was with the foreman at a building site. He slipped, crossing an I-beam that was suspended seventeen stories up at the time. He only survived because he happened to land on an elevated platform several stories below. He was wearing a hard hat, but he still fell a long way.

The first time Mom took me to the hospital to see him, his head was bandaged and he had casts on an arm and a leg. It must've been soon after it happened. I sat on her lap across the room from the bed, and she whispered in my ear that Daddy was going to be all right.

I don't know if she believed it.

I SPRAWL AWKWARDLY in the vinyl chair beside Dad's bed. My right leg sticks out straight, while my left knee hooks the armrest. My bare toes rest on the edge of his mattress. My left arm's in my lap, and my right arm trails out of the chair, almost brushing the floor. I rest my neck on the chair back.

This bizarre position is really comfy to me now. This is how I always sit when we talk. I stare at the ceiling; it's just easier for me that way. There's this weird green smudge on one of the ceiling tiles. I've spent hours, maybe days, inventing ways it could have gotten up there. It's a problem I really need to get to the bottom of, before . . . I just really need to get to the bottom of it.

"Dad, this whole situation is really fucked up." One of the things I love about Dad is that there's no need to censor myself around him. I can be real.

"Mom wants to turn off your machines. Can you

believe that? I told her to shove it. Well, I didn't say 'shove it,' but you know what I mean."

Dad's hand twitches.

"I know, right?" I say. "Like I'd ever let her do that to you. Anyway, she won't do it unless I say it's okay. She promised. So we're fine. You don't have to worry about anything. You're not worried, are you?" Maybe I shouldn't have brought this up.

I look at his face. Eyes closed, lips a little bit parted. Very dry looking. I reach for the jar of Vaseline on the nightstand and smooth some over his mouth.

"Sorry I can't stay," I say, rubbing my hand over the scratchy top of his head. The nurses have buzzed his hair close, and recently. "Mom'll find out if I skip again."

RUSHING OUT OF ALF, I pass Dad's day nurse, Carmen, in the parking lot.

She raises a brow at me. "Hi, Ellis. Cutting it close for school, eh?" She glances at her watch.

"Whatever."

"You need a ride?"

"Nah, bus," I say, waving toward the stop. Who cares if I'm late for school?

Carmen looks me up and down, repositions her

bag on her shoulder. Her scrubs are a bright, friendly purple. "Oh, c'mon." She shrugs. "Shift doesn't start for ten minutes. I'll drive you."

I dutifully follow her to her car, a beat-up two-door sedan with low bucket seats. We ease in, and she starts the engine, zipping right out of the space as she's snapping her seat belt into place. I love that she doesn't comment when I don't buckle mine.

"You sure this won't make you late?"

"No worries," she says, artfully gunning across four lanes of traffic to catch the right turn arrow. It yellows as we sail on through.

"Well, thanks."

"Morning visit," she says, eyes on the road. "Anything going on?"

Pause. "Was it you who cut his hair?" I ask.

Carmen makes a face. "Too short, right?"

"Definitely."

"So much for my second career as a hairstylist." She dials up the volume on the radio. "I love this song." It's a croony love ballad that makes me want to gag even while I hum along. We rock, heads bobbing to the beat, until the car pulls into the bus lane at my high school. I hop out, minutes to spare before the bell rings.

"Catch you later," Carmen says.

"Yeah, later."

3
Colin

We both cling to our obsessions.

THE LAST DAYS of school are the most painful. I can
practically touch the edge of that summer euphoria—
the ice-cream-truck, bike-to-the-beach, sleep-till-
noon liberation high that comes on the heels of the
rising heat and humidity. Close, but not close enough.

I slam my locker, wiping sweat from my brow as I
meander down the hallway toward whatever is first.
Social studies?

My skin is slick with the inevitable perspiration.
The sun steams us through the windows, turning our
no-AC classrooms into greenhouses. The teacher has
two fans pointed toward her desk, stacked textbooks
tamping down all her piles of papers. Great. She'll be
looking windblown, talking over the hum, while the
rest of us swelter.

Abby is already there, sprawled in a seat at the center of the room, working her electricity on poor Colin. Short and wide, with comically thick glasses, Colin Conner hovers on the verge of any number of unpopular groups: nerd, geek, reject, loser, loner. But he has a quiet power that has allowed him to rise to be one of the in-crowd. Strings attached.

Abby smiles up at him amid a feline stretch of her perfectly shaped arms. Colin's cheeks are flushed red, his armpits stained with sweat, but he's rapidly fanning Abby's exposed throat with a worn notebook.

"Oh, Colin," I say to this pathetic specimen. "Have you no pride?"

His fanning arm works faster than ever. Colin has the biceps of a Greek god and the belly of a Buddha. We're not sure how such a quirk of physique is possible, but Abby exploits it at every opportunity.

She grins at me and reaches beneath her desk for a second notebook. Colin automatically takes it in his hand and begins to fan me, too.

It feels damn good, but I roll my eyes.

"Colin, get a life." I grab the notebook from him and smack him on the back of the head. The notebook lands with a splat on Abby's desk. She shrugs, closes her eyes, and leans back into her personal wind.

Colin shoots me a dirty look. I set my books down

on the desk next to Abby. Colin has already claimed the one on the other side. I sigh. I love this kid. He's wonderfully brilliant and equally deranged, but he has a profound weakness: Abby. He can't resist her, and she knows it.

I grab for the other notebook, temporarily freeing Colin from his chains.

"Hey," Abby complains. "What gives?"

"Fan yourself," I tell her.

Colin mops the sweat from his brow. He catches my eye and shrugs one shoulder at me—half grateful and half annoyed.

"Colin doesn't mind, do you, hon?"

"Of course not," he pants. "What are friends for?"

COLIN AND I are the first to reach our lunch table. We sit at the end of one of the long rectangular tables, mostly talking to each other even as the table fills up with the rest of our group. Sometimes Abby sits right next to us; other days she holds court more toward the middle of things. Last year I tried to instigate a move for just the three of us to one of the small round tables nearby, but Abby said those are for the losers without many friends. Colin even came down on my side for a while, saying if we played it right, we could make it a status thing: *Look who's cool enough to sit at Abby Duncan's table.* Turns out, what Abby loves is not the exclusivity, but the crowd, and where Abby goes, Colin follows. So we're back. It doesn't make much difference to me, in the end. Sitting in silence among friends is better than sitting alone.

I pick at my à la carte salad, watching Colin watch Abby approach us. She stops by the jocks' table, tossing her perfect caramel hair and smiling in what Colin once called "a kissable way."

When Mom finally let me straighten my hair last year, I practiced tossing my hair like Abby for hours. I've got it down now, but it's a skill I rarely have the opportunity to use.

Dennis North, the wrestling team captain (talk about the body of a Greek god . . .), actually stands up to flirt with Abby. She tips back her head as they laugh, and Dennis manages to touch her shoulder, stomach, and ass before the joke has run its course.

Colin toys with his fork. Usually, he's not one to delay any kind of ingestion.

"You okay?"

He can't tear his eyes away. "Sure. Yeah."

We figure Abby to be the second most popular girl in the sophomore class. She's standing there in a ragged sweatshirt and simple jeans, but every jock at the table is checking her out. She's that girl.

Abby wants to be everywhere at once, it seems to me sometimes. For Colin and me, there's nothing to do but wait for her to circle through our midst. He lives for these moments, and it's written all over his face.

"It's going to happen one day. Me and her," Colin declares, plowing into the Salisbury steak on his tray.

"Hmmm." I don't have the heart to tell him that Abby doesn't see him. Not really. Even if he had a chance, it wouldn't be good for him. He would be trampled, and he'd go down smiling.

"My mom wants to do it," I tell him. "To end it."

I surprise myself, blurting it out like that. I hadn't meant to tell anyone. Not yet.

Colin's chewing slows. "Yeah?"

"Yeah." I do feel a bit relieved, having it out there. I tear at my lettuce slowly, still not hungry, but it feels like the breaths I'm taking are deeper. More calm.

It's funny that it's Colin I can talk to. We've only been friends since mid-freshman year, and Dad had already been in ALF for several months at that point. Colin wasn't around when the accident happened, doesn't know the whole story firsthand, only the things I've told him. There's a certain look he gets on his face, though—a look that says he knows what it feels like to hope for something that's not even remotely in his hands. I see it when he's thinking about Abby.

"Wow." He's paying attention to me now. For the moment, Abby is forgotten. "What are you going to do?" he says.

I shrug. "You got any ideas?"

"Wait and see. Maybe it'll blow over again." Colin, the optimist.

I draw my fingers through my hair. "Not this time. It's different."

"How do you know?"

"She sat me down to *talk*."

Colin raises his brows. "And you talked?" Colin knows what it's like at my house, though I still haven't told him about the dream.

"No, I kinda stormed out. But she said—"

Abby slaps her tray down across from me. "He didn't even ask me to the dance. Can you believe it? After all that." She drops into the chair.

I blink toward her, untangling my mind from my own problems. "What?"

She waves her hand, impatient. "Dennis. God, he's so dense. I even told him I'm free next Friday, and nothing. Can you *believe* that?" With Abby, there's always lunchtime drama. Today, I'm really not in the mood. I let my forehead drop into my hands.

"The graduation dance, remember?" Abby persists, prodding me with her fist. "I'm dying for him to ask me. And we have to get you a date, too."

"We're sophomores," I remind her. "Don't get your hopes up."

Abby rolls her eyes.

"Maybe you should ask *him* out," Colin offers, picking at his slice of soggy Jell-O cake. I slide my glance toward him. He is the best friend either of us could ask for. Sometimes I don't know why Abby and I bother with each other.

"Yeah, like that's going to happen," Abby said. "Guys are supposed to chase *me*."

"He wouldn't say no, if that's what you're worried about," Colin says, suddenly scarfing the cake. He defends himself with helpful comments. Today, it's making me sick.

Abby flips her hair. "Of course he wouldn't say no. That's not the point."

"Oh," Colin says. "Well, anyway, you should be with somebody who gets you." He moves his tray back and forth in front of him.

"No, I should be with someone *hot*," Abby says, laughing.

I can't take it anymore. "If he's so dense, why do you even care?" I say. "Dennis is a jerk. I don't know what you see in him anyway."

Abby rolls her eyes. "You wouldn't."

"What's that supposed to mean?" I push my salad away.

"You don't know what it's like. You never go out with anyone." Ouch. True, but still. My face grows hot.

"I mean, why won't you at least try to get a date for the dance?" she whines.

"Maybe I don't want to."

"Whatever, Ellis."

I spin the salad bowl round and round. "We were having a *conversation* here, you know. Before you sat down."

Colin intervenes, T-ing his hands like a referee. "Guys, stop it." He puts his hand out, touches my arm. "Ellis."

I jump up from the table. "I don't want to talk anymore."

Abby's voice follows me. "What's her problem?"

I don't hear what Colin says in response. Maybe he tells her. Maybe he doesn't. But he'll say something. Colin will always find words to say to Abby. And even if he knows I need someone right now, he will not come after me.

4

Goldfish Crackers

They remind me of being little.
Long before anything changed.

I BUY A PACK of Goldfish from the snack cart and head out to the courtyard. The problem with storming off from one's established lunch table is then you have to find another place to sit. Either that or wander around looking too cool to be held in one place or to be seen associating with anyone. I'm fairly sure I can't pull off the latter.

I take a casual stroll around the yard as if I'm stretching my legs. Most everyone else is seated, so I kinda stand out. I need someone—anyone—I can sit with. Someone slightly less popular than myself, someone I won't be embarrassed to approach, but not so uncool as to be disreputable. The thing is, there are three or four tables inside where I could easily sit. But as soon as I do, someone will start a round of gossip about why I'm not in my usual seat.

I could just go back. But I know that when Abby's in the mood she's in and I'm in the mood I'm in, we always end up in a fight. I know I'm spoiling for something right now, but it really isn't that.

I tug open the little foil package in my hand. Goldfish were perhaps not an inspired choice for this moment. I savor their light flavor and crunch, but they're really not the kind of food I can escape into. They make me think of how, when I was a kid, I'd throw them and Dad would try to catch them in his mouth. Then he'd caution me never to try it, because I might choke. He never worried about himself choking. I wonder, did he worry about falling?

The courtyard is pretty quiet, just the hum of cars from the street beyond the building, and a few quiet, wafting conversations. I'm a bit surprised to realize most of the people out here are eating by themselves.

Cara Horton's sitting high on the concrete steps to the auditorium, alone, a giant sketch pad open on her knees. We used to be friends, Abby and Cara and I, in middle school. We're still technically friends, I guess. There was no big, dramatic end to things. Cara just drifted away from us. Maybe we never were

very good friends in the first place, if something like
that could happen.

It seems way weird to go up to her now. After so
long. I can't even remember the last time we spoke,
let alone hung out. I know it was sometime after Dad.
Cara was with me that week, when it happened. The
week of May 10, spring semester of eighth grade. We
were all at Abby's house, painting our toenails, when
her mom came in and said I had to get in the car with
her and go to the hospital. I remember how we didn't
know yet what was going on, but Abby insisted on
coming along. She and Cara threw themselves into
the minivan and refused to move, even though her
mom said no. I remember their faces, wide-eyed and
trying to smile, even though we were all scared, sitting in the waiting room those first few days, holding
hands. Then the summer unfolded, and after a while,
I was still waiting there, but Abby and Cara were not.
Abby resurfaced at some point, I guess. On the first
day of high school, she and I went arm in arm, but
Cara was gone.

Will she even remember, or care?

At the moment she's my best bet. I climb the
steps.

"Goldfish?" I stick the pack out toward her.

"Huh?" Her eyes are outlined with deep green eye

shadow. "Oh, hi, Ellis. No thanks." She's working her way through a serious pile of carrot sticks. She's extracted them from their plastic bag and stacked them like Lincoln Logs on top of it. She crunches on one, looking back at her drawing. I feel like she wants to be left alone.

"Well . . . sorry to bother you."

She smiles, lifting her head again. "No bother."

This is encouraging. "Could I maybe sit down for a minute?"

"With me?"

"Is it okay?" I nod toward the cafeteria. "Just needed to get out of there. Away from . . . stuff."

"Yeah?" Cara looks me over. "Yeah. How is 'stuff' doing? I heard she broke it off with basketball player number a zillion last week."

I grin because I can really use some Abby-deprecating humor right now. "The wound has healed. She's moved on to wrestlers."

"Naturally."

I sit down on the steps beside Cara and help myself to one of her carrot sticks. The little smile that touches her lips brightens her whole face.

She bends her head over her notebook again, and I remember that she's shy. I don't know how I forgot that.

I look over her shoulder. The work is familiar, but better. Her art is really weird. I always liked it, though. She does these little geometric shapes in all kinds of patterns, like mosaic tiles or M. C. Escher tessellations. She thinks they aren't really art, but I can picture them in a museum or gallery, or someplace like that. Maybe on fancy greeting cards or T-shirts. Except Cara wouldn't go in for anything as cheesy as that, I suppose.

"I miss your drawings," I say, realizing that it's true. Lately I'm so wrapped up in my head that it's hard to remember what things were like before I got to feeling so screwed up all the time. Cara makes me remember those easier days, when all we did was laugh and play and Dad always came to pick me up after. I don't even know how everything changed. It's like I woke up one day and suddenly there was this weight upon me that I couldn't shake off. Maybe it started the first time Mom said we were going to have to let Dad . . . go. Maybe it started when he fell. Maybe it's always been there. Hovering over me, waiting to come down.

Cara puts her arm around my shoulder, probably because out of nowhere, I am crying. Not loudly or embarrassingly, just a couple of tears leaking down the sides of my face.

She kind of hugs me from the side, leaning over her carrot tower until we are pressed close together. Her head is on my shoulder, and it makes me so glad, more tears come. When she sits up, she watches me with quiet concern.

I scrub at my cheeks. "Sorry, that was totally weird."

"Nah," she says.

The warning bell rings. Five minutes to get to our next classes.

"Sorry," I repeat, leaping to my feet so fast I fear I may have just flung myself down the stairs. I catch my balance, but the stab of terror leaves aftershocks coursing through me. I can't get away from this feeling, not waking, not dreaming. I shut my eyes and try to pull it together.

I face Cara, and smile as politely and normally as I can. "We should hang out again sometime."

Cara looks up in alarm. I kind of choke on a laugh because her expression is so utterly desperate.

"Yeah, never mind. You probably think I'm a freak now. Forget it."

"No, no," she says. "But just you and me, okay?" She says it in this closed-off way that makes me look back, trying to remember what happened, why we really stopped hanging out. I get nothing.

"Sure. Well, see ya."

"Ellis?"

I turn back. "Hmm?"

"It's going to be okay."

"What is?"

Cara shrugs, half smiles. "Whatever."

RIGHT AFTER SCHOOL, I head for ALF. I sit with Dad for an hour, eating Goldfish and not saying much. It's been the kind of day where I just want to see him. To know that he's there.

Mom will probably be upset, but I don't really care. She doesn't like how much I come here, thinks it isn't good for me, though she hardly ever comes right out and says it. Instead she bakes cookies and spreads out pamphlets that say things like "letting go is healthy." Maybe, finally, she will get mad and yell at me, forbid me to come here instead of asking nicely. I'll refuse, of course, because I'm old enough to do what I want. We'll have it out, and then I'll feel better.

WHEN I EXIT ALF, Colin's waiting. I cross the grass to the bench where he's sitting, his head bent over his U.S. government textbook.

"Only losers hang out at the nursing home," I say.

Colin slaps the book shut. "Oh, this is a nursing home? Shit. I came to audition for *American Idol*."

"Seriously, what are you doing here?"

He holds up his textbook. "Some truths are self-evident."

I snort. "Not that self-evident, apparently, or that book would be a lot thinner. What, you couldn't think of a better place to read up on checks and balances?"

"Thought you could use some moral support."

Did I mention I love this kid?

I open my arms and spin around. "What, am I, like, wearing a banner that reads 'lonely, pathetic, and desperate'?"

"Actually, it just says 'pathetic' right now, but I can order you a new one."

I shoot him a withering look. "Wow, I'm feeling so supported."

Colin jumps up and scrambles my ponytail. It's the kind of touch that makes it super clear that we are just friends and only ever will be, but at the same time makes me wonder what it would be like to have someone I could be more than friends with.

I body check him, throwing my whole weight behind it and nearly toppling him over. I am shortish, but not small. He circles round and headbutts my backpack. This goes on for a few minutes, until we're both laughing and gasping for breath.

Colin snags the package of Goldfish crackers from my pocket and polishes them off. "This is not going to cut it," he says. "Let's get food."

"I want a milk shake." Let Mom wonder where I am a little longer.

But first I have to know if he said anything to Abby. "Um, about earlier. . . . Did you tell her?"

Colin looks honestly dismayed. "What do you take me for?"

"Just checking. Thanks."

Sighing slightly, Colin slings an arm around my shoulders and leads me away from ALF.

5

Warm Chocolate Chip Cookies

For that one second when you bite into
their tasty, melty, gooey goodness . . .
nothing hurts.

THE COOKIES ARE WAITING when I get home. Six of
them. Arranged on a neat little plate.

"Was your bus running late?" Mom says as I dig in.

I plow through two cookies before replying. "What,
you want me to lie to you now?"

"I'm trying to give you the benefit of the doubt."

Mom does that thing with her hands that means
she wishes she had a cigarette—something to take the
edge off. It's a little flutter of her fingers as they move
from item to item on the table, but nothing's what
they are searching for. She quit smoking two years
ago because I asked her to.

She quit once before, while she was pregnant with
me. She told me she'd done it for me once, and she'd
do it for me again. I think maybe it was a lot to ask,

this time around. Considering all that she has to deal with.

I down two more cookies. Her hand flutters. At times like this, I see her in a different way—almost like not my mom. I see her young and restless, looking for something to burn. I wish I could have known her as a teenager. Someone I could relate to. Be honest with.

She takes a cookie and nibbles its edges.

"I'm not sorry," I say. "At least he understands me. Anyway, what do you care?"

"He doesn't understand anything, Ellis."

This is such a tired old fight that it has no impact left.

"You don't know him like I do anymore," I blurt. "You never visit him."

Mom brushes her fingertips along her hairline from ear to ear. "I want you to talk to someone," she says. "I made an appointment."

"I'm not going to any more doctors." I can't abide another stuffed-shirt know-it-all who wants to dig inside my head. It's futile.

I liberate the last cookie. Warm. Soft. Perfect.

"Honey." Mom gives me the look.

I look back. "Mo-om."

She clears away the cookie plate. It clatters into

the sink. "She's different from the others, I think. I saw her yesterday. I've met her a couple of times, actually. I think you'll like her."

"I'm going to my room now." I slide off my stool.

"I worry about you, you know." Her words, light as air, float after me down the hallway.

AT TIMES LIKE THIS, I leave the door open, just to see if Mom will come in. Just to see how far she'll press the issue. It's never very far.

Mom stays in the living room all evening, while I sit at my desk doing my homework.

I get good grades. Straight A's, actually. I'm sixth in my class, as of now. I don't think of myself as really smart or anything, but I work hard. I have to do something to occupy my mind, so it might as well be something productive. Dad was valedictorian of his high school class, Mom told me once, so I always make sure to tell him how I'm doing in school. I know he's proud of me.

That's one of the things the last shrink never got about me—how I can do well in school and still be a total wreck. I guess he thinks that messed-up people aren't usually academically inclined, but I like to bust the mold.

After a while, I lie on my bed listening to Mom get ready for work. She runs the shower and listens to ABBA while she does her makeup. I catalog her mood by the CD she chooses. ABBA means she's feeling hopeless and needs to be cheered up.

There's been a lot of ABBA lately.

I want to roll over and tuck my head under the pillow so I can't hear her worry. So I can pretend that I'm all alone. But it's the two of us, always. I can't forget about her.

I hear the off-and-on rush of the faucets. The zipping and unzipping of makeup pouches. The hum of the hair dryer. The whisper of drawers. The scratch of hangers sliding along the rod. The hiss of a licked thumb on the hot iron.

Mom appears in the doorway pressed and dressed. She looks nice. Professional. I wonder for the millionth time why it matters what she wears. No one can see her.

"I'm leaving," she says. "Good night."

"Okay, Mom."

I ALWAYS SAY I won't go to the new doctors, but I always end up going. I don't know why. Mom's wrong about it helping. One time, though, one of the shrinks had me close my eyes and make a safe place in my mind. It's a meditation thing that apparently lots of people are into. Whatever. I tried to make a joke of it, but in the end I actually liked it.

We never went back, because I told Mom he was creepy (he was), but the place I made . . . it follows me. I slide into it sometimes, by accident mostly, when I can't handle myself, my thoughts, the world. It's quiet there. The air is filled with small-feathered birds. Their wings flit against me. My skin grows damp with dew that smells clean and perfect.

In my quiet place, there's no such thing as sleep. I stay wide awake, and the sky swirls in sweet pastel hues. Days stretch on into infinity, and the silence is so beautiful and deep, I cannot even carry one thought in my head.

When Mom's gone, the whole house falls into per-fect stillness. The walls breathe a sigh of relief, for no longer having to contain us both. They fold around me, a cocoon woven of all the things unspoken. I walk through the rooms, appreciating the air, the space, the silence, pushing any still-hanging words out of my path.

The world is out. I am in. It's my quiet place come to life.

6

Mrs. Scottie

When she holds you, you know
it'll be all right in the end.

AT PRECISELY TEN THIRTY P.M., the front door clatters
open. My respite is over.

"Hello-o!" Mrs. Scottie calls. Slippered footsteps
travel the hall. She appears in the living room, clad
head to toe in flannel, clutching her plastic bucket of
yarn. "Ellis, dear, it has been a whale of a day."

"Hi, Mrs. Scottie. What's new?" I sit up on the sofa,
putting the TV on mute.

She plants herself in the recliner with a graceless
flop and digs into her yarn. Wads of blue, black, gray
come out in a knot. Her fingers untangle the strands.

"Three rubbers in, do you know what that old bat
Lillian Wattlesford said to me?"

I giggle. I can't help it. I know she's talking about

her bridge game, but hearing Mrs. Scottie say "rubbers" will never not be funny.

Mrs. Scottie frowns, peering at me over her spectacles. ("We drink out of glasses, Ellis, dear. We see out of spectacles.")

"No," she says. "No, on second thought, I mustn't corrupt your young ears."

"My ears are old enough."

"Umm-humm," she says, extracting two long thin needles.

Mrs. Scottie comes over every night at bedtime. Technically, she lives next door, but on the nights Mom works, Mrs. Scottie stays in our spare room.

I tell Mom all the time that I'm old enough now to go to sleep without someone watching. She smiles and says, "That's true." But Mrs. Scottie still comes over.

"And how was your day?" Mrs. Scottie says, though I'm dying to know what that old bat Lillian Wattlesford said.

I lie quiet for a moment.

"No rubbers at all," I quip finally, grinning.

Mrs. Scottie click-clacks away at her knitting. "As it should be, dear. As it should be."

AT MIDNIGHT, I go to my room. Mrs. Scottie's relaxed my proper bedtime, since she knows I'll work myself up if I have to lie in bed too long before I'm actually tired.

I click on the radio, which I keep set to Mom's station. She's talking now. That's all the show is about. Her talking. She plays a little music from time to time, real soothing stuff that calms people down, but it is her voice that listeners tune in for.

People all over the city fall asleep to the sound of Mom's voice. So many letters came in when she dropped from six nights a week to five that now the station replays her old recorded shows on the weekend.

I leave the door ajar because Mrs. Scottie is out there, even though I pretend not to be soothed by the click of her knitting needles in the living room.

I snuggle down beneath my comforter, but Mom's voice is my blanket. Tonight she's talking about loss. The ache and the emptiness. The screams and the weightless fury. The part of you that never really believes.

The mellow, drawn-out sadness of her words leaves me with a bit of a chill. It happens this way sometimes. I wait it out, until the words blur together into the simple noise of her, and at last I grow warm.

I wonder if she knows I listen. If she is ever talking just to me.

MRS. SCOTTIE POKES her head in the door to check if I'm sleeping. I relax my jaw and make slits of my eyelids.

Slippered feet cross my bedroom floor. With a familiar quiet sigh, she turns off my bedside lamp. The tiny night-light in the corner grows brighter.

She stands for a moment, leaning over me. Her breath smells of butterscotch candy. When she pulls back and slips away, I celebrate my minuscule achievement with a twitching of my toes.

I never know if she's really fooled.

7
Abby

For better or worse, my best friend.

WHEN ABBY CALLS the next evening, I'm lying on my bed with my feet in the air, waiting to see if they will get pale in addition to tingling as all the blood drains away. My phone rings, and my experiment is ruined.

I roll toward my desk. The little screen glows ABBY.

I can pretend I'm not around, but then she'll just call the house. Answering is inevitable.

"Hi."

"Dude. What gives?"

I roll back into legs-up position, like a flailing insect on the kitchen floor.

"Are you mad?" Abby says into the silence.

"Kinda."

"What'd I do?"

"I don't know."

"Oh." Long pause. "Well, do you want to come over?"

Why? is what I want to say. But this is what we do. "I guess."

"Okay. Come soon," she says and hangs up.

I clap the phone shut and chuck it toward my back-pack. It's Friday night. I shouldn't spend it caging myself in my bedroom.

I jam a pair of sweats and a baggy T-shirt into my bag. I throw in a couple DVDs, all cheesy-ass come-dies where nobody gets sick or dies. I slam the desk drawer hard enough that the broken heart pinned to my bulletin board jumps on its chain. Mine is ST NDS. Abby's is BE FRIE. I kind of like her half better, which is dumb.

We don't wear the necklaces anymore, because we're too old and too cool for that stuff, but I kept mine. It's supposed to be a forever thing.

"I'M SPENDING THE NIGHT at Abby's," I say, bounding into the kitchen. I plant my butt on the table, stretch-ing my feet so their tips rest up on the counter next to where Mom is reading a recipe.

She peers at me over her shoulder, then opens

her mouth, I'm sure to tell me I'm not going anywhere. But she says nothing. Instead, Mom nips at my toes with her knuckles.

This is one of the moments when I remember that our relationship is a flawed and fragile thing.

"If it's okay with you," I add, in a semipathetic mumble.

"Go ahead," she says. "Have her mother call me, please. And don't forget to tell Mrs. Scottie."

MRS. SCOTTIE'S HOUSE smells like malted milk. Always has and probably always will. Mind you, I've never seen her drink a malted, but that's just the way it is.

I step onto the porch we share and knock on her door, knowing full well she'll be out. Mrs. Scottie is always home when I need her and never around when I don't. It's weird. (This is not even an exaggeration—it's scientific fact. For nine months I kept the statistics.) She does rummy on Mondays, bingo on Tuesdays, and bridge on Thursdays, each with a different group of friends. I think it's canasta on Friday. Wednesdays she gets her hair done.

I scribble a note to her and leave it pinned between the screen door and the jamb:

Staying at Abby's tonight.
Hope you won big today!
xo, Ellis

Tonight, Mrs. Scottie gets to sleep in her own bed, and I get to sleep in Abby's.

ABBY ANSWERS THE DOOR swaddled from neck to ankles in her fluffy yellow bathrobe, her face a Cheshire grin. Right away I know I've misjudged what this evening will entail. *Shit.* I didn't think this through.

Abby's mom is lying on the sofa with her feet in Abby's dad's lap, and they're watching television.

"Hi, girls," Mrs. Duncan calls as we snake past them through the living room.

"Hi, Mrs. Duncan." I smile. She blows me a kiss over the back of the sofa. It lands exactly on my cheek. Nice.

"Don't bother us," Abby grunts, unnecessarily. Her parents are sharing a bottle of red wine and a platter of Sun Chips and carrot sticks. Before the clock hits double digits, they will both be zonked out and snoring in those exact spots. Comfortable.

"My mom wants you to call her."

Abby disappears down the hall, but I linger in

the living room. The quiet warmth calls to me. A sit-com laugh track echoes over us. Mr. Duncan laughs along with it.

"I'll do that," Mrs. Duncan says. "At home or at the station?"

I shrug.

She reaches over the back of the sofa toward me. I drift closer and let her smooth her fingers along my hand. "How are you doing, sweetie?" she says.

Abby pokes out of the hall. "Ellis, come on."

"I'm fine." I duck my head and trail Abby to her room, where she slams the door like it means something.

"Sorry. They're such losers," she mutters.

"Hmmm." Actually, her parents are kind of cool. I would tell her so, but she won't see it because she'll never know what she has until it's gone, and I know the Duncans well enough to know that for Abby it will probably never be gone, so it's a point I don't bother to make anymore.

Abby locks the bedroom door behind us. My back-pack bounces off the edge of her mattress as I toss it toward the bed and turn in time to face the big reveal.

Abby peels off her bathrobe the way models shed fur coats at the end of the runway. She doesn't throw it over her shoulder, though—she loses a few style points as she simply tosses it aside.

"What'd you do to your boobs?" are the first words out of my mouth.

Abby beams. "Good, right?"

She's wearing a miniskirt that is all mini and almost no skirt, and a deep V-necked halter featuring seriously impressive cleavage that is not at all representative of Abby's budding B cups.

"Yeah, it looks good. What's in there?"

Abby smirks, spinning with her arms out. "Trade secret."

"Oh, come on. You know you're gonna tell me." I flop down on her bed, propped by a mound of sparkly turquoise throw pillows.

"First touch them and tell me if they feel real."

"Oh, please. I'm sure they're fine." Checking Abby's stuffed boobs for realness is not my idea of fun on a Friday night, but I know I must take steps to stall what is inevitably coming next. Dreading the answer, I ask "Who else is going to be touching your boobs tonight, anyway?"

Abby grins in a way that I know all too well, the way that means I should really just have stayed home and wallowed in my various miseries instead of trying to cheer myself up by joining the land of the living.

"I don't know yet," she says. "I'm hoping maybe Dennis?"

Oh, great. "Dennis?" I echo, helpless. No way to elude the drama that's to come, might as well run headlong into it. "Since when?"

Abby looks in the mirror, adjusting. "We walked between two classes together yesterday. I dropped a book in the hall, and he picked it up and then I was just . . ." She shakes her hands wildly. "He's so cute!"

"Uh-huh."

"If he doesn't take me to the dance, you're going to have to kill me," she wails.

I resist the urge to roll my eyes. "Don't say that."

"Just do it. C'mon. Feel." She thrusts her chest toward me.

"Fine." First I grab my own boobs—which I'm not ashamed to say are fairly generous—for a control group. Reaching forward, I cup hers.

"Well, they feel . . ." I'm really tempted to lie. Send her back to the drawing board and delay whatever foray into the world of Dennis she's planning. But I'm tired. I don't want to have to sit here trying to come up with better boob ideas. I was doomed the moment I walked in the door, so whatever it is, let it come and let it be over. "They feel pretty darn real. What is it?"

"Jell-O Jigglers in Saran wrap."

The image that pops into my mind is Dennis, horny and trying to get past second base, lowering his lips to Abby's chest and coming up with a mouthful of lime gelatin.

I cover my laugh with what I hope sounds like an impressed chuckle. "Wow, that's . . . creative."

Abby pulls her makeup crate from under the bed as she launches into explaining the genesis of her Jell-O boobs.

I dig back into the pillows, trying to listen. Her chatter swirls around me, but I only grow heavier and heavier in this spot, like I will never be moved. Abby's craziness usually has the ability to take me out of myself and make me forget stuff, but this is not helping. I randomly point to purple when she asks what color eye shadow, and she nods like this is an inspired choice.

I wish she would just look at me, look at my face and stop talking long enough to see me. To see that things are not right. That none of this is real and I am in some other place.

"Now, what are we going to do about you?" she says, raising her eyebrows at me.

"I'm fine," I say, pretending she has bothered to ask what's wrong.

"No," she says quietly, and for a second I think it'll be okay to tell her.

"The jeans are okay, but you at least have to change your shirt," she says.

I am so erased from this place. Abby's talking to a great big blur, and I'm desperate to know why she can't see that.

"I didn't bring a change of clothes." Everything Abby owns will be too small for me, so she has to let me off the hook.

I'm wrong. She throws me a tube of fabric. Could be a skirt, could be a top, but in its unworn state, it resembles one of my pant legs. "I can't wear this."

"Sure you can. It's stretchy."

I strip off my T-shirt and tug the silvery tube over my boobs and my belly. It squeezes, but at least it reaches the top of my jeans, hiding all of me inside. A major relief, because I refuse to do bare midriff. I step over to the mirror. My boobs are pushed together in rather a nice way, I think, but then I rethink, and actually the cleavage is kind of overdramatic.

"I look ridiculous."

"You look really good," Abby says. I look at her looking at me in the mirror, and I'm tempted not to believe her because she has ulterior motives, but one thing she does not do is lie about when people look good. She can't lie, because the jealousy gleams in her eyes, and I can see it—and it lifts me up a little, even though she's prettier than I'll ever be.

"Thanks," I say.

Luckily, my bra is the kind with straps that unhook. I stuff them into my backpack. Then it's like a blade of scissors runs over a ribbon and the whole of everything curls up inside me, and I can't stand up anymore, so I kind of fall onto the bed.

"I don't want to go out."

Abby grabs my arm and pulls. "No! We have to go. Please, pleeeeeeeaaaaase."

"I can't." Everything but my eyes is crying, *Don't make me.* But Abby is dressed and ready, and she has put Jell-O in her bra because that's how badly she wants Dennis to touch her boobs, and who am I to stand in the way of that? If Abby believes it to be just another Friday night, maybe at some point the feeling will rub off on me.

I climb off the bed and put my best best-friend face on. "Okay. Sorry. I'm really tired."

"Oh, we won't stay out long," she promises, still gripping my arm. This is a transparent lie, but I shrug and pop *Ferris Bueller's Day Off* into her DVD player and pump the volume just high enough so that when her parents wander off to their bedroom later they'll hear it and think we're in here having fun.

"Thank you." Abby hugs me, unexpected and strange, her hands on the bare skin of my back and her Jell-O boobs pressing against me.

"Yeah, yeah." I let her hug me, closing my eyes. Maybe underneath it all, she senses I'm having a bad day.

"Really," she says, grabbing my hands and starting up our old, secret BFF handshake. The one we made up together, long before boobs and boys and parties. If we could get back there, I think, everything would be okay.

Abby grins as our fingertips bounce off one another. "I love ya."

"I know."

I do know. Abby will bribe me with love, because somewhere deep she knows it's what I crave, and I'll go with her, because, damn it, that's what craving makes you do.

8

The Dark

There's something perfect about not being able to see too far ahead.

THE WEATHER IS IDEAL, a thick, unsticky heat that makes you feel like you can get away with anything. I poke my head out Abby's bedroom window and breathe it in.

The lights on the street and in the house windows make it undark, but the swell of shadows is enough to hide some things, which is how I like it.

Abby returns from the living room. She relocks the door, once again shedding her thick robe. I pull my head back in.

"They're soooo asleep." She rolls her eyes. "Never even saw me."

With a triumphant smile, she extends the mug in her hand toward me. *"Cabernet Sauvignon,"* she declares in an elaborate faux French accent: *ca-bur-nay so-veen-yon!*

I sniff it and nod approvingly, although it smells like car tires. "An excellent year."

"Go ahead. You can drink first," Abby says.

I stare into the mug. The wine has sloshed up on the edges of the white ceramic, leaving little purplish trails. "That's okay. You can have it."

"Really?" Abby takes a long sip, makes a face, then holds it out to me again. "Are you sure?"

"Hey, it's only fair. You did the recon." Abby has become expert at sneaking the right amount of wine from her parents' bottle after they fall asleep. There is always leftover, and they never notice any missing.

"But you'll have something later, right?"

"Sure," I say. "Later."

"Cool." Abby steadily chugs the wine, draining the mug to the dregs. She wipes it out with a tissue and shoves it under her bed, to be snuck into the dishwasher later. She reapplies her lip gloss, then extends the tube to me.

I slide a layer of Watermelon Slick over my mouth, because it doesn't hurt to dream, most of the time.

Abby tucks the gloss into her waistband and hands me the Purse, for which I am now responsible.

It contains all the necessary items: our cell phones, our learner's permits, our money, Tic Tacs, my house keys, hair ties, a spare gloss, a compact, and tissues.

We open the window wider, and Abby is feeling the wine already, so I try to hush her giggles as we climb into the undark. I would like to feel relieved that we're out of the house, out of the light, where I don't have to feel like anyone should notice anything out of the ordinary. But instead I feel a sense of rushing, rushing toward the rest of this night, and I don't like the sensation at all.

Abby grabs my hand. "Come on." And just like that, we are hurrying, racing, skipping across the yard away from the house.

"COME ON," Abby says, trying to hurry me up. She sings, "I wanna go to Grover's!"

"It'll still be there when we get there."

"Ellissss," she pleads, running ahead. There must have been more wine in her cup than I thought, because she's giddy as all get-out.

Grover's Field is a popular weekend hangout spot for kids from our school. The proper name of the complex is President Grover Cleveland Memorial Athletic and Recreational Acres, but who has time to say all that?

Abby lives near the north edge of Grover's, but the Field is way to the south, so we have to cross through the rest of the park. The sports fields are fenced off after dark, but the playground and picnic area is wide open at all hours.

Grover's is dimly lit, but not seedy, not the sort of place where you have to be nervous to go at night. We go tripping between the fences, me because I'm dragging my feet, and Abby because she's tipsy. Maybe she snuck a beer from the garage and drank it before I got there.

"Is Colin meeting us there?" I say.

"Not coming tonight. Family thing."

"Ah." Suddenly my role in the evening crystallizes. Abby is going to get wasted, and it'll be my job alone to drag her home. I don't know why this didn't occur to me before.

It will cost us five dollars each to party on the Field. Some of the seniors use fake IDs to buy kegs of beer, or else they get their older brothers or uncles or someone to buy it. I've gone to the party a couple of times before, but Abby usually goes alone with Colin. It's easier that way, for all of us. Colin gets to be with

Abby. Abby gets to be wild, knowing Colin will always be right there to keep her out of trouble. I get to avoid all superfluous human contact.

We hear the others before we see them. Abby loops her arm through mine as the shape of the gathering looms up out of the night. The cars are driven up right onto the grass, in a loose circle. Abby makes a beeline for the keg, which is propped in the bed of a black pickup that belongs to one of the football players.

I pay ten dollars to the guy in the letter jacket who's guarding the stack of Solo cups. He draws a star on my hand with a Sharpie and stares appreciatively at my chest. Suddenly I'm very aware of my outfit.

Abby sticks her fist out for her star, and moments later, we're both clutching big blue cups of beer.

"There he is. I see him," Abby says, casually nodding toward where Dennis is standing, chatting up two girls from the volleyball team.

"Well, you better get in there," I say, nudging her toward them.

I lean against the hood of someone's car and try to look casual. A cute senior guy smiles at me on his way over to the keg, tossing me a saucy wink and finger guns. I blush a little; my own personal here's-looking-at-you-kid moment. I wave to a couple of girls that we're friends with, but they're busy hanging with their boyfriends, so I'm not going to go over and make myself the fifth wheel. Tonight I'm thinking unicycle.

There's no one else here that I care about in the slightest. I'm just going to sit here, hold this beer, and wait for Abby. She's made it over to Dennis. I hope she gets what she wants quickly so that we can go home.

Abby likes the parties, but really she likes the drinking. She says it makes her feel strong and alive. I've never asked her why she lies. When you stand at the edge, it's obvious who's sucking down beer for the fun and the feeling of it, who's doing it because of peer pressure, and who's doing it out of pain. I just don't know what Abby has to be worried about. Everyone likes her already. I swirl the beer in my cup until a little sloshes over my hand.

Looking around, I start the game of guessing who's having fun, who was dragged here, who felt pressured into coming because it's the cool place to be. These are the small things I do to pass the time, but also to prove that I'm better because I know when I'm being manipulated. I could stop it anytime.

Anytime.

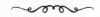

ABBY'S LAUGHTER is impossible to miss. She has him to herself now. Dennis drinks from his cup. He nods at whatever Abby is saying, but he's looking over her head, and if I didn't know better, I'd think he was looking at me. But it's dark, and the shadows are getting the best of me.

Dennis saunters toward me, Abby close on his heels. Then he's at my side, resting his hand on the hood of the car near my hip.

"You paid your five bucks," he says. "Are you going to waste it staring into the same beer all night?"

"Could be," I say, tossing my head so that the breeze lifts my hair away from my face. I catch Abby's glare out the corner of my eye, and every good thing I should do for her right now flies out the window.

Dennis taps the bottom of my cup with his fingers and lifts it toward my face. I can see his eyelashes and smell his breath.

I take two slow sips of the required beer. Dennis is close, watching. Actually he's looking straight at my chest. I wonder if my boobs move when I swallow. I sip, then lower the beer to shield my cleavage from his gaze.

He flicks his attention to my face. The grin is taunting, telling me I am not good enough. Well, maybe I'm not. Maybe I don't care. I stare until he starts to grow uncomfortable.

His face curls with mocking pity. "Looks like we've got a lightweight," he says loudly, looking my body up and down so that nobody misses the irony. Chuckles echo from among the faceless crowd.

I just stand, looking at Dennis. I don't really care that he's mocking me. Maybe I should worry about it, I don't know, but he's an asshole, and it seems so insignificant in the face of everything else. If I just stand here, say nothing, after a while he'll lose interest and I will win. I can win this. His cheek twitches, and I am moments, seconds from victory.

Fuck it. I chug until I'm staring at the little plastic imprint in the bottom of the cup. SOLO. The jocks stomp their feet and cheer. When I stick out the cup for a refill, Dennis nods like he has been proven wrong, which he has. Someone pumps me a fresh draw from the keg and I suck it down to a rousing chorus of "Chug! Chug! Chug! Chug!" SOLO. I lift the empty cup high in triumph. There is another cup ready for me. Dennis is close now, very close, and he pushes the new beer at me in such a way that his knuckles graze my breasts and kind of linger. I grab the cup away and step back. It's Dennis, for God's sake. Dennis, who I hate and Abby wants. Why does it have to be Dennis?

Abby steps around near to me, but nearer to Dennis, her body aligned with his, and I know she has not come to save me. Her eyes are alive, and the spite in them is aiming at me.

"Whoa, Ellis," Abby says, her voice a little slurry. "Fast track to the whiny-winey-witching hour?"

Everybody laughs. My cheeks flame. That is supposed to be a private joke, and not a very funny one, at that.

Abby puts her hands up. " 'Cuz y'all haven't seen what Ellis is like after too much beer."

If I thought I could throw a decent punch, I might slug her.

"Shut up," I say, which I should know won't help matters. I have crossed the line—a couple of lines now—and Abby's staking her claim. I know better. I do. Abby wants to look good, to be seen, to have all eyes on her, and here I am letting the jocks incite me to chug. Letting Dennis look at my boobs, which are actually real. Stealing her audience, when I don't even care. I get that. It's my bad.

"I'm finished, Abby," I say, holding up my hand. "Do you wanna go next?"

The pause is long enough that most everyone moves

on. They start shifting and chattering in the background, a dozen conversations that have nothing to do with us.

"No, I think you should keep going," Abby says quietly, draping herself over Dennis's arm. The Jell-O boobs have his attention now. "Keep going, so they can all see what a baby you really are."

I sip the fresh beer in my hand. The only other thing to do is cry, and that would only make Abby's words true.

"We're just having a little fun here," Dennis says awkwardly.

"You're soooo right," Abby says. She comes up on her tiptoes and says close to his ear, "I'm having such a great time. Can I get another beer?"

"Sure, yeah. Good idea." Dennis's hormones have kicked back in. He hurries to the keg and pumps two full cups.

Abby stands staring at me, waiting for him to return to her, which of course he will, and that's all she wants. Loyalty is second to the limelight in her eyes. But I don't want to be center stage. She can have it. It's okay with me. It's really okay.

"Bitch," I mouth at her before I turn and walk away into the dark.

9
The Swings

Sometimes it's the simple things.

I AM SORELY TEMPTED to leave Abby there. Just take the Purse and go. It's within my power to do that, and it would serve her right. She chose Dennis over me and probably won't look back, so I don't owe her anything. Not tonight.

The problem is, where would I go? It's a twenty-minute walk to Abby's house, but if I'm ditching her, I don't want to be in her bedroom when she falls in the window later, drunk as a proverbial skunk. We will fight, and her parents'll hear us and then we'll both be in a world of trouble. But my house is another twenty minutes beyond Abby's, and do I really want to go all the way back there, when I'll have to explain to my mother in the morning how I ended up in my own bed? On top of which, I've had better than two beers, one right after the other, and don't really feel much like walking anywhere.

I promptly sit down, somewhere in the middle of the Field, hoping I'm far enough away from the others that they can't even see my shape poking out of the grass. The last cup of beer is still in my hand. I set it aside, half empty. SOLO. I lie back on the ground, which is just a touch cooler than the air and feels refreshing on my skin. Solo.

I'm not drunk, but I feel something kind of like drunkenness coursing through me. It's still good and soft, though, which is how I know I'm not drunk. I got drunk once, guzzling stolen wine coolers with Colin and Abby. I will never repeat it, never, ever in my life. Just to think of how it felt makes me shiver in place—a miserable, unsteady feeling, like suddenly it seemed possible to fall off the earth. I spent sixty-two minutes screaming and crying and clutching the grass before finally passing out. Colin calls it my whiny-winey-witching hour, but when he says it, it's not unkind, just something we all know and share. When he says it, it's never cruel and in public.

I hear footsteps slushing along the field. My heart flutters with the stupid, stupid hope that Abby has come to find me, bearing apologies.

"Ellis?" I know the voice, but it's not Abby's.

"Cara?"

"It's me. Hi."

"What are you doing here?"

Silence. A large silence, which my rudeness swells to fill.

"Sorry, I didn't mean to imply"—*that you aren't popular enough to be invited*— "I mean, I shouldn't have— You can be anywhere you want, of course."

"I wasn't offended." She sighs as she settles into the grass beside me. We stare at the sky, the faint dots of stars that are visible through wisps of clouds and above the ambient glow of all the distant streetlights.

"Why do you tolerate her?" Cara says to the sky.

"She's my best friend."

"Is she?"

"I just said she was." I'm irritated by her skeptical tone.

"Okay, sorry."

The air is peppered with lightning bugs. My gaze flits from one little burst to the next. I try to predict where they will appear.

"What are you really doing here?" I ask. "This doesn't seem like your idea of fun."

Cara sighs. "It's complicated."

"What isn't?" I mutter. My slight buzz is fading, and I'm glad to see it go.

"Sometimes I go to the swings," Cara suggests. "To get away from everyone."

"No, I like it here," I say. It is on the tip of my tongue to ask why you would come to a hangout place if you wanted to get away from everyone, but then again, who am I to judge?

"That's cool," she says. "I don't know why, anyway. I guess the swings make me feel like a kid or something. Like nothing matters."

I would speak, tell her that I'm touched by what she's said, but I can't. A memory of Dad rises out of nowhere. The strange, uncomfortable quiet between Cara and me carries me back, far back, until I'm held in his arms.

We play on the swingset at Grover's. He pushes me, but I've learned to pump my legs, and so I want to do it myself. Swing, back. Swing, back. "Too high, Ellis. Too high!" His voice floats, but I am flying, laughing, so when I crash into the gravel, I am shocked. I cry. My knee is scraped open, and the palms of my hands sting.

Dad scoops me into his lap, kisses the back of my hands. I bounce in his arms as he runs to the car. He sets me down and fumbles for the first aid kit. He pours alcohol over my knee because he doesn't know about peroxide and that it hurts less but still kills germs. I scream. The Band-Aid is

tight and sticky, then he hugs me, and I know there will be
a chocolate milk shake coming.

I remember.

The tears run out of my eyes into the grass. It aches and it aches, but I remember. For the first time in a long time, I remember. Thank God that it's dark so Cara can't see, for the second time today, what a freak I am. The stars blur, and I'm just grateful not to be alone.

"I changed my mind." I sit up, feeling dizzy and waiting for it to pass. "Let's go to the swings."

MY FEET DRAG in the gravel. A reassuring sound.

Cara, on her own swing, leans back, straightening her arms, relying on the plastic-coated chains to keep her hanging in midair. She points her toes.

I watch her, loving that she doesn't seem to care that I'm watching. Her black hair streams away from her face. There is just a hint of a breeze.

"I'm not going to finish this beer," I say. "If you want it." The cup is perched on the ground near the swingset pole.

"No, thanks. I'm going to be driving."

"Oh. You have your license?"

"It's complicated." Her body is an almost perfect plank, feet higher than her head. She's trusting the swing, the air, the earth not to hurt her.

I bury my toes among the tiny stones. "But you know how to drive already?"

"Yeah, well, Evan taught me."

I nod. I guess these are the advantages to having an older brother. "He's a senior now, right?"

"Yeah. Mr. Big Stuff."

"That must be nice." I can't imagine how it would feel to have someone else my age around the house. Would we sneak into each other's rooms to talk late at night? Would we go together to visit Dad? Would he side with Mom and want to . . . ? No. He would always have my back.

Cara snorts, coming upright. "Nice? Not really."

"Oh."

"It used to be cool, I guess," she says. Maybe she senses my disappointment. "But right now, he's just mean."

"Oh."

"Yeah, like, he makes me come here even though I feel like a total loser around these people. No offense."

"Oh, please. I feel like a loser here, too," I admit.

Cara laughs. "Hmm. But it's not the same. You're popular."

I tilt my head. "No . . ." Being friends with certain people hasn't made me popular, not really.

"Yes, you are, Ellis," she says. "Hello, Dennis North was hitting on you a little while ago." She nods toward the group. "*They* don't think you're a loser."

I shake my hair over my face, wanting to change the subject. "So why do you come, then? Evan can't really make you, can he?"

Cara sighs. "Sort of. It's a quid pro quo thing."

I feel it's my duty to repeat the phrase in the proper Hannibal Lecter whine. "Quid pro quo, Cara?"

She grins. "Yeah. My parents worry because they think I don't have any friends. I don't get out enough, etc. You wouldn't believe some of the things they've tried to get me socialized." She rolls her eyes.

"So Evan, brilliant deductive mind that he has, figures out a way that we can pull one over on them. Now, when he goes out, I go out. He and his friends get bulldozed, and then I drive them all home."

"But you don't have your license?"

"Just my learner's. That's why it's a secret."

"Why would you do that?"

"He gives me money for art supplies."

"Ah."

She shrugs. "I get paid to suffer public humiliation; he doesn't die or go to jail. QPQ."

"And, so you're, like, cool by extension?"

Cara laughs. "Not hardly."

THE DANCE MUSIC is pumping. They've turned on more headlights. The deep gray air has turned murky. We are better than shadows now, silhouettes. A lone figure weaves her way across the grass toward us.

Cara says something under her breath. I would ask her to repeat it, but we are no longer alone.

"There you are!" Abby throws herself into my lap. The swing rocks as I fight for balance. "Where have you been?"

She kisses the side of my hair. I can almost hear her buzzing.

"I've been here," I say. I hold her waist to steady her, but I'm uncomfortable with her on top of me. She might want to just blow past everything that happened earlier, but I'm not going along with it.

"Dennis is soooo hot," she groans, swaying against me. "We totally made out."

"Good for you."

Suddenly Abby is looking past me.

"Oh, God," she says. "What are *you* doing here?"

Cara taps her chin. "Having a wonderful time. Wish you would leave," she chirps.

Abby's eyes narrow. "You don't belong here. *You* should leave."

I stand abruptly, dumping Abby on her ass in the gravel. She sits there stupidly, gazing up at me. Cara fights back laughter, covering it with a little cough.

"Ellis?" Abby's voice is puzzled. She reaches her arms toward me.

"Dennis is coming," I say, nodding toward his approaching shadow. "I'm sure he'll be *glad* to help you up."

10
Cara

For being everything Abby is not.

I STALK ACROSS the grass in a wide circle, veering far from the cars and the people into the deeper shadows along the grove of trees. Cara follows my hurried steps.

"I don't need you to defend me to her," she says out of nowhere.

I stop walking. "I wasn't."

"Sure seemed like it."

"No. I'm mad at her about something from earlier." About this whole damn night, really. If only I could erase it all and go back home. I'd tell Abby no when she asked me to sleep over. I'd lie in lonely agony on the living room couch while Mrs. Scottie knit beside me.

"I heard what she said to you, you know."

I scoff. "Yeah, and I'm sure no one else did. She's so soft-spoken." The sarcasm tastes good.

"Friends don't treat each other like that."

"Shut up, Cara. It's a fight. People fight. Friends fight."

"I'm just saying—"

"You don't know what she's like."

"I know exactly what she's like," Cara snaps. "Better than you. Don't tell me I don't."

I'm shocked by Cara's venom toward Abby. And curious now about the bitter history. But my head is swimming with fury. I can't bring myself to ask.

"You don't know!" I blurt out. "You don't know anything about it."

"So tell me!" she says.

But I can't. I can't say any more about it. I waste the days trying to talk but not saying anything. I spend the nights trying to forget but not forgetting.

"It's none of your business," I whisper. Every trace of the fight has gone out of me. I turn back toward the party. The pulse of the music is steady. Familiar. I'll go dance along with everyone else and paint a smile on my face. Let the headlights blind me to everything but the hopping bodies all around.

She grabs my wrist. "What's going on? Is it Abby? I don't think it's Abby."

"I want to go back to the party." I tug my hand free, leaving Cara behind.

Her voice, so quiet—almost far away—follows me. "Ellis. How's your dad?"

It occurs to me then, with blinding clarity, that I have never been asked. No one asks about my dad. Everyone knows, but no one ever asks. Have they all forgotten? Do they just not care?

"He's dying," I whisper to the vacuum of the air. "And there's nothing I can do."

CARA'S HUG IS LONG and warm, so different from anything I have ever felt. I can't even cry. We sit in the grass again, facing each other. Almost knee-to-knee.

"I've missed you," she says.

"Me too." It's truer than I've realized.

I gaze across the dark grass toward the party in its circle of light. If coming to Grover's always meant easy, quiet, hanging with Cara, I'd come a lot more often.

We sit without speaking, which is a huge relief from everything. She threads her fingers through the grass, letting the blades slide between them gently. I copy her motions, not as graceful, of course, but the silky cool whisper of grass against my skin is soothing. From time to time, our fingers brush.

"Did you mean it?" she says. "About us hanging out?"

"Yeah."

She reaches for the Purse and extracts our cell phones, mine and Abby's. "Which is yours?"

"That one." I point.

She slides the screen up and taps along the keypad for a while.

"What are you doing?"

"Nothing." She smiles and closes the phone. Slides it and Abby's back into the Purse. "Well," she says. "This was fun, but I have to go home now."

"This was fun?" I echo wryly. The sting behind my eyes has come and gone, but still.

Her laugh is sweet. "Well, you know what I mean."

The party's breaking up. The twelve-thirty curfews are starting to pull out.

I search across the lawn for Abby, and I can see that something has changed from the usual. She's draped across the hood of Dennis's car. He's leaning over her, working to replace her clothing, which has partly been removed.

I've left her alone too long. I can see that she has

taken herself beyond caring, and I don't like the stabbing I feel in my chest knowing that I'm partly to blame for hurting her. It's past time to go.

"I'd love to see you leave her here," Cara says wistfully, and again I'm sorely tempted.

"I want to."

"But you won't," Cara says, and after a moment adds reluctantly, "You shouldn't."

What goes unsaid is that I would never. Not in a million years.

"Come on," Cara says. "I'll drive you home."

ABBY TURNS HER HEAD away from me in the car. Whatever. She can slight me all she wants.

We're squished into the front seat of Evan's Jeep Cherokee. Cara's driving. I'm straddling the gearshift, and Abby is spread over Evan's and my laps. Her body is loose and malleable, and she can't seem to keep her limbs reined in.

This is by far the quickest my ass has ever fallen asleep.

The four guys piled in the back seat are being loud, drunk, and annoying. They spew off-color comments and apparently find each other hilarious. One of them haphazardly offers to take Abby off my hands.

Somehow, she finds the wherewithal to flip him off over my shoulder. The others howl.

Evan reaches between us, ostensibly to adjust Abby, but he sure enough gets a handful of my boob.

"Oh, sorry." He smiles apologetically, but doesn't move his hand. "Stuck," he says. Abby's shoulder is pressing on his arm. A likely excuse. I can't push his hand away; my own arms are trapped. I roll my eyes, biting back the retort that pops into my head. At the moment, I'm willing to overlook his piggishness because the alternative is me dragging Abby down the road under my own power.

How much longer? I focus on the passing street signs. CLINTON BLVD. GRAYSKILL AVE. Uh-oh. "Hey, you missed the turn. Abby lives back off of Edgewood."

Cara's attention is on the road, but she makes no move to correct. "I said I'd drive *you* home," she says.

"But I'm staying at Abby's."

"Sorry, I don't have time to swing out to her place," she says. "Yours is on the way."

This is bad. Bad, bad, bad bad bad. Bad. We can sleep at my place, no problem, but what will Abby's parents do when they find out we snuck out and then stayed out all night? This is not how it was supposed to go down. Abby's going to be furious when she realizes what's going on.

Cara pulls into my driveway.

"Well, thanks for the ride," I say. I mean, I really am grateful.

"Anytime." She smiles. "Talk soon?" Her voice is quietly hopeful.

"I'd like that."

Evan gets out and pulls Abby after him. When he tries to stand her up, it doesn't go so well. The guys in the back seat guffaw at her unsteadiness. I throw the Purse over my shoulder and scramble out to catch her, but Evan's already there.

"I'll help you to the porch," he says, leading Abby that way. His arm is locked around her waist, keeping her upright. All the while, he's looking straight at me.

"You look nice tonight, Ellis."

"Huh?" I blame the beer glow in his eyes. And my slightly slipping tube top.

Evan leans forward and kisses my cheek. Out of the freaking blue.

"Good night."

"Um . . . good night. Thanks."

"See you." He strides back toward the car.

The Purse vibrates under my arm. Abby leans on the door frame while I dig for my keys, and for whichever of our phones is ringing.

It's mine. The little screen glows CARA.

im so sorry. stupid drunk boys.

After everything, my quick, deep smile is unexpected. So that's what she was doing before—getting
my number and programming hers into my phone. I
text back quickly:

its ok. not ur fault.

I wave to her through the windshield, but it's Evan
who waves back.

I vow never to wear this kind of shirt again.

11

My Own Bed

Even when I can't sleep, I'm glad to be in a place I feel comfortable.

WE MAKE IT as far as the living room before Abby says, "Uh-oh."

I dump her on the couch, grasping for something . . . anything . . . the big bowl of potpourri petals so dried now it's hard to imagine they are giving off any scent at all. I thrust it under Abby's chin.

Nothing happens.

Maybe it was a false alarm—nope. Here it comes.

She pukes hard into the bowl.

"Okay, come on." I help her up, half leading, half dragging her to the bathroom. She sits on the floor. I get a wet towel, some dry towels, just lots of towels, really, to cover the cold tile.

I'm not ready when the second wave hits. Abby misses the toilet entirely, and it lands on her leg, her skirt, and one of my fresh-laid towels. I simply ball the towel up and stuff it in the trash. There's no way I'm cleaning that. I'll sneak it out in the morning.

I tie back her hair and push her closer to the toilet. She rests her cheek on the seat.

"How do you feel now?" I ask. I've been to parties, but I've never seen anyone this drunk before. I doubt Abby has ever been this drunk before. It was annoying in the car, but now that we're alone, it's a little scary.

"Hmmm?" Her eyes are closed.

I lean closer. "Abby? How do you feel?"

"Why did we have to leave? I was having fun."

"I know."

"You don't like it when I have fun."

I clear her bangs out of her eyes. "That's not true."

She laughs, and it echoes off the porcelain. "Yes, it is."

"We have fun together, though, right?" But even as I say it, I'm racking my brain to remember the last time we did.

"You don't even like me," she says.

I stare at her. "Abby, we're best friends."

A little tear slips out from under her eyelid. "I don't feel good."

"I know." I start undoing her clothes, which smell like vomit. We get her out of her skirt and shirt, so she's sitting there in panties and a too-big bra. Something's wrong with this picture.

"Umm, Abby, what happened to your Jell-O?"

She looks at me blankly for a few seconds. Then she starts laughing. "Oh, I got hungry."

I cough. "Excuse me? What?"

She laughs, falling onto the floor. "I got hungry, so I took them out."

"Are you telling me you *ate* your fake boobs?"

She nods.

I'm horrified. "Not in front of Dennis, I hope."

"Dennis," she sighs. "Yeah, we ate them."

I start laughing, too. I can't help it. "Oh, my God. You are deeply disturbed."

"I feel better," she says suddenly, sitting up straight. "Oh, but it's spinning." She lays her head on my lap. "Ellis."

I stroke her hair. "It's okay, Abby."

"I want to go to sleep."

"Let's just stay here a little longer," I say, not totally convinced.

"Um-hmm."

I fluff the towels into a little mound for her to rest her head on. "Here."

"No, no, don't go." She pulls at me, practically climbing me. "Just hold me so it doesn't spin," she says.

I ignore the abject irony that brings the night full circle. After all, she's my best friend and she needs me.

I WAKE UP because I have to pee really bad. My head's buried in a mound of towels. Abby's lying all but on top of me. I squint into the bright overhead bathroom light, groaning in sudden discomfort.

"Abby."

No response.

"Abby." I poke her in the side. "Abby, you gotta get off me."

She's breathing into the side of my neck. I try to move, but end up wedged between the bathtub and Abby.

"C'mon." I nudge harder. "I'm gonna pee on us."

"What?" Abby mumbles. She shifts her legs just enough that I can slip out from under. She lands face first in the towels, murmuring, "Hey."

"Sorry, go back to sleep."

"Hmmm." She curls up into a ball and drifts off.

The sound of the toilet flushing doesn't even stir

her. I snap off the bathroom light and pad down the hall to my bedroom.

OF COURSE, once I'm in my bed, sleep doesn't come so easy.

There's a whole catch-22 playing out in the back of my mind. I can almost feel it tug-of-warring. I don't want to lie awake, but sleep is the danger zone. I don't want to think, but more than that, I don't want to dream.

I wish hard for the dawn, try not to look at the clock. Mom's voice on the radio tonight just reminds me that I've screwed up and there's trouble coming along with the light.

Still, the covers soften around me, draw me into their cocoon.

"Just let go," Mom says to the caller on line three. "It's time to just let go."

THE TOILET FLUSHES.

Thud.

"Oww."

I sit up in bed. Abby appears as a looming shape in the doorway, rubbing her elbow.

"How's come we're at your house?" she muses, climbing into bed with me.

"Don't ask."

Her presence jolts me wide awake. I was actually asleep just now, I'm pretty sure.

"Are you still feeling sick?" If she pukes in my bed, I might seriously kill her.

"God, did I really pass out on the floor of your bathroom?" she groans. She curls tight under the sheets, putting her back to me.

"Good a place as any."

"Hmm . . ." And with that she's breathing softly. I snuggle back down, looking for comfortable, finding nothing that's even close.

THE ALARM CLOCK buzzes early, six thirty. I don't want to go anywhere but back toward sleep. We have to get to Abby's, though, before her parents think to miss us. And out of here before my mom gets home, which could be any minute now.

Abby brushes my hand off her shoulder. "Sleep, sleep."

"Come on. Get up."

She rolls over, moaning. "What's your problem? It's sooooo Saturday."

"We have to get back to your place, ASAP."

"Oh." She sits up slowly, cradling her head. "Oh, not good."

"I'll get you some Advil. Find something to wear."

We keep Advil and twenty million other over-the-counter drugs in a basket under the bathroom sink. Something for every occasion. We're big on pain relief around here.

I return to find Abby staggering out of my bed, clad only in bra and panties. I gasp. "Oh, God." Her chest is spotted with little purple bruises. "Are those hickies?"

"Oh, God!" Abby echoes, poking herself. "I think so." She leaps to my wall mirror for a better look.

"What were you guys doing?"

"I don't know." She tugs at her flapping bra cups. Then her hands fall to her sides. "Did you take out my . . . padding when we got back?"

Oh, no. Oh, God.

"No. Abby, you told me . . . wait, what exactly happened between you and Dennis?"

She shrugs. "We were dancing. Making out. We sat in his car for a while. Whatever."

"What did you do with him? Exactly."

She glares at me in the mirror. "I don't know, Ellis, okay?"

"Are you being generic, or you really can't remember?"

She says nothing, but comes to sit on the edge of the bed. I sit with her. "Oh, Abby."

"It's not a big deal." She takes the Advil from my hand and swallows it dry.

"Um, but you didn't . . . ?"

"I don't remember," she says sullenly. "I really don't."

"Abby." I reach out my hand to maybe touch her hair, her shoulder, I don't know, but she pulls away.

"I was wasted, okay? Whatever." She's back in front of the mirror. "If he kissed me here, he could have seen the Jell-O."

She doesn't know. I have to tell her. "Abby, you told me you ate the Jell-O. With Dennis."

"Yeah, right."

My shoes are on and tied, and she's still in her underwear. "I'm just telling you what you told me. Now, get dressed, we have to go."

"You're lying," she says. "There's no way I would do that. I was going to sneak them out if we were fooling around. I had a plan."

"Like I said, I don't know for sure."

"Oh. My. *God.*" Abby's pacing around the room. In a second, she'll start throwing things. She digs in my dresser, then my closet for something that'll fit her.

Six colorful T-shirts fly toward me before she decides on the one that says MAC TONIGHT.

"Not that," I snap. She sticks her arms into it anyway.

"I'm just borrowing it."

"Not that!" It's the shirt my dad gave my mom when they were dating. She gave it to me after he got hurt.

Abby's wearing it now. "What? It's not like it fits you, anyway."

"Take it off."

Abby rolls her eyes. "Get over it. You can just bring it home with you after we get back to my place."

"It's mine! Don't be mean, just 'cause you got stupid last night. Don't take it out on me." I try to pull it off her, but she fights away my hands.

"*I'm* being mean?" Abby knocks me onto the bed. "It's your fucking fault I can't remember!"

"What? It so is not!"

She stares at me accusingly. "Colin doesn't let me get this wasted."

"Colin's a sucker."

"I'm telling him you said that."

"No, you won't. Because he's not an idiot. He'll

demand to know the context. And I'm sure you'll agree that's a story best left untold."

"Well . . . well . . ."

While Abby searches for her comeback, I stomp to the dresser and dig out one of the bold-print wrap skirts that I never wear. When the drawer slams, my picture frames rattle. Dad smiles from one. Another has Abby and Colin and me with our arms around each other. The third is a promo shot of Mom at the station, headset on, leaning into the mike, smiling.

Abby jumps in surprise as the wrap skirt flies into her face.

"Put it on. We're going."

12

Riding the Bus

There's something soothing about motion.
It allows me to almost forget.

"THIS IS THE WORST hangover ever," Abby groans. We wait for the bus at the end of my street. In the space of that three-minute walk, she seems to have revised her current opinion of me.

I can't say the same.

"Just shut up, okay?"

"Okay. But my head hurts. And my stomach." She hugs one of my arms in both of hers and leans her head on my shoulder. I let her.

Five seconds later: "Are you still mad?"

"Yeah, I'm fucking mad, okay?" We're dealing in truth this morning.

"Don't be mad," she says. "You know I'll give the shirt back. But you have to help me figure out what to do about Dennis."

"What?"

"This is, like, the worst thing that could possibly happen."

"I can think of worse things."

She tugs my arm. "I'm serious. What am I going to do? I mean, what if he *tells*?"

"That you stuff your bra? Big whoop. I think half the sophomore girls do."

"It's embarrassing," she whines.

The bus turns the corner, coming our way. "I don't think he'll tell. He probably wants to go out with you again."

"Really? Did you think he was into me? Like, for more than one party?"

She may be cutting off circulation to my arm. I shake her loose and swipe our fare cards, and we settle into a double seat.

"Was he looking at me different? What did you see, I mean, how was he acting toward me? Tell me everything!"

"I didn't really notice."

"Come on, Ellis . . ."

The city glides by out the window and all I want to do is watch it pass in silence.

"I'm, sorry. Abby, I don't think I can deal with

this right now." If you can't be honest with your best friend, who can you be honest with?

Abby studies me with something resembling concern. "Our fight's not over yet, huh?"

"I just have a lot of stuff on my mind."

"I'm sorry I yelled at you," she says, fingering the hem of my Dad-Mom-me shirt. "I'm sorry. I just—I thought you'd have my back. You know, at the party."

"Well, don't count on me, okay? Maybe I'm not that good of a person. Maybe I don't always know what to do."

Abby reaches past me to signal for our stop.

"No one's perfect," she says.

THE BUS STOP is just around the corner from Abby's house. We hurry down the block and come around onto her street, big as life . . .

And shit if her dad isn't already out and trimming the hedges.

13
Getting Away with It

It's fun. No other reason.

WE PRESS OUR BACKS against the side of Mrs. Rabbins's house like super-secret spies. Two houses away, Abby's dad works the electric trimmer along the bushes. The soft whine of the motor buzzes lightly through the air.

"What's the plan, Stan?" Abby whispers.

"I don't know, Joe," I say, feeling the barest hint of a smile, our fight laid aside in this moment of desperation. We must, must, must get into Abby's house unseen.

"Time check?"

I consult my cell phone. "Seven forty-five."

"We're so fine," Abby says. "They won't expect us to even be awake for another two hours, let alone to emerge from my room."

"Yeah, but we still have to get in there. How long does it take your dad to trim the hedges?"

Abby groans. "Not long, really, but he could stay outside for hours. Puttering in the tool shed or mowing the lawn or whatever. He won't go in till he's hungry. Something about being cooped up in his office all week long."

"So we need stealth, yes?"

"Definitely."

"Okay. Thoughts?"

"We left my window unlocked."

"So we know our point of entry."

"Affirmative."

I can't help but grin. I feel like we're little again, playing CIA in the backyard. I guess, in crisis, we revert to the familiar.

"So, let's get to the other side of the house and then regroup."

"Yeah, okay." Abby peels out. Staying low, we scurry toward the hedges at the side of Mrs. Rabbins's lawn. We hop from yard to yard, skirting widely around Abby's house so we are sure to stay out of sight of her dad.

Soon enough, we are crawling along the edge of Abby's next-door neighbors' garden, partly shielded by a decorative grape arbor. We hide and wait. It must've sprinkled overnight. The air is earthy, the ground a bit damp.

"When he's done, he'll put the trimmer away in the shed," Abby says.

I nod. "That may be our best shot."

Abby lies flat out in the dirt. "Can you keep watch, please? I don't feel good."

"Yeah." I try to ignore the fact that she's muddying my shirt. But I can't. "Get up. Don't get my shirt dirty."

"I'm sick. It'll wash."

There are a thousand things I could say, a thousand things I'm thinking, but there's no time. The trimmer motor cuts out. Peeking past the arbor, I see Mr. Duncan heading toward the shed at the back of the yard.

"Come on." I nudge Abby. In ten seconds . . . nine . . . eight, he'll disappear from sight.

"Ready? Go, go!"

We dash across the lawn, holding back our breath and trying not to laugh aloud, lest he hear us and come investigate. Who knows how long we have.

My hands grapple with Abby's window ledge; I still have one eye on the shed. The open door blocks me from seeing in, which is great because it also blocks Mr. Duncan's view out.

We get the window open. Abby dives in headfirst. I'm right behind her, landing practically on top of her when I fall inside.

"Shhhh . . ."

We pause, listening. Then we let ourselves collapse on the floor, and we're choking back hysterics because we have lived the dream and gotten gloriously away with it.

From above, Abby's mom says, "Girls, we need to talk."

14

Getting Caught

It's always a bit of a relief.

MRS. DUNCAN'S SITTING on Abby's bed, cross-legged and cool as a cucumber, browsing a stack of Abby's magazines.

We are so busted.

Abby sits up. "Mom! This is *my* room. What are you doing? Go away!"

"Abby, this is *my* house. I enter whichever room I wish, at any time that I wish. And I expect the people who are supposed to be in that room to be there when I stop by."

Mrs. Duncan tosses the magazines onto the floor where she probably found them. She looks at Abby for a long moment. Then me. I swallow hard.

"Living room. Two minutes. Both of you." She sweeps out the door.

"We're not coming to the living room," Abby shouts.

"I'm getting your father. We'll see you in two."

ABBY AND I slump on opposite sides of the living room couch. Mrs. Duncan plants herself between us. Mr. Duncan sits in one of the two armchairs, laying his yard gloves on the coffee table. He strokes his neatly trimmed beard.

Mrs. Duncan looks from me to Abby, but for some reason settles on me.

"Are you all right?" she says, quite warmly.

"Fine."

She turns to Abby. "And what about you?" Her tone sharpens a little.

Abby makes a face that would wither flowers.

Back to me. "Mrs. Scottie called to tell us where you were."

I'd been wondering how they found out. We were quiet when we left, sneaky when we came back. They shouldn't have suspected a thing.

Enter Mrs. Scottie. I sink deeper into the couch. I can't believe she ratted us out. I'm not surprised that she found out—she probably heard us coming in last night—but why would she go out of her way to call the Duncans? I'm steamed.

Mrs. Duncan's still talking. Something about what is and isn't acceptable behavior. We get it, already.

"Ellis, we've spoken to your mother." Mrs. Duncan's gaze turns sickeningly sympathetic. "We know this must be a very difficult time for you. You're in a fragile emotional state, so it's understandable that you might act out—"

"All we did was go to my house," I say. "What's the big deal?"

"Let me finish, hon," Mrs. Duncan says. "I know this must be difficult for you to deal with, but this isn't the way to handle it."

I see what's happening. They're going to blame all this on me, on my situation and my *fragile emotional state*. I glance at Abby. She stares at her socks.

It's like she doesn't care. She doesn't ask what the IT is that's supposedly so difficult for me. Or maybe by now she's guessed. She presses her toes together innocently, and I think that maybe she's about to let me take the fall.

How far would she let it go? I don't want to know. I step into the pain.

"I'm sorry," I say, letting my voice shake. "I just wanted to go home to my own bed. Abby felt bad letting me go alone, when I was upset."

Mrs. Duncan's expression softens. She reaches to pat my knee. "Oh, sweetheart."

"We didn't want to wake you. We thought we'd just go and be back before you ever missed us."

"You could've left a note," Mr. Duncan grumbles.

"Yes, but it's simply not safe for two young girls to be roaming the streets at that time of night," Mrs. Duncan says.

I wonder what time of night she's imagining.

"I'm sorry," I say again.

"Yeah, we weren't thinking," Abby pipes in, finally.

"Well, you'll have plenty of time to think on it now, young lady. You're grounded. No phone. No computer, except for schoolwork."

"Dad," Abby whines. "We didn't do anything."

His forehead creases sternly. "You think I don't know a hangover when I see it? I was young once."

Abby flops back deep into the couch cushions with an aggravated sigh. She crosses her arms in a petulant display that makes no difference at all. Mr. Duncan has spoken. It is what it is. Grounded.

The doorbell rings. Mrs. Duncan slips into the hall-way and returns moments later, trailed by my mother.

15
Mom

*I do love her. A lot. I just
don't always know what to say.*

THERE ARE CIRCLES under Mom's eyes. She comes in
carrying nothing, no purse, bag, or briefcase, and
she seems to me strangely empty. She perches on the
edge of the waiting armchair, looking everywhere in
the room but at me.

Her eyes linger on the shirt Abby's wearing—my
shirt, Mom's own shirt—for a long moment.

"Mom, what are you doing here?"

It's past her bedtime. I've pulled us out of the
routine. She tugs on one of her fingers, finally studies my face.

"I came to pick you up," she says. "Mrs. Duncan
called, and I was worried about you."

It's what she has to say, in front of the Duncans.
But I read the lie in her eyes. A stretching of the

truth, at least, because she wasn't there to worry. She had no idea anything was up until they called her.

"I'm fine," I say, brushing a stray hair from my eyes. We are very good at saying things that people want to hear.

I glance at Abby. She now has on her bulldog face, which means she's about to dig in and make this a fight to end all fights. For her, an all-points grounding is the worst of all the worst possible punishments.

She's staring at me, waiting for me to jump in and help her out. Nothing between us is forgiven, but she's calling for my help to fight this conspiracy of grown-ups to make our lives a living hell.

I can't help her now. I'm afraid. I'm afraid because I've suddenly realized that, with all that's happening with Mom about Dad right now, grounding would be the worst of all the worst possible punishments for me, too.

IT'S STICKY HOT and quiet in the car on the way home. I clutch the Mac Tonight shirt and my wrap skirt in my lap, picking off flakes of drying mud. Mom says nothing, and I don't know whether to be relieved or terrified. *I have to be able to see Dad* is all I can think.

"I don't know what they told you, but it wasn't my idea," I say as we walk from the driveway into the house. "Abby wanted to sneak out, not me. Really."

"I believe you," Mom says. She opens the front door and sends me through ahead of her.

Mrs. Scottie's sitting in the living room. Knitting.

"What's *she* doing here?" The traitor.

"Ellis, be polite."

I whirl on Mom. "Are you going to ground me, or what?"

"No, I'm not going to ground you."

"Why not?" I should be relieved, but instead I feel this trembling ache. There's supposed to be yelling. There's supposed to be punishment. There's supposed to be some sign that when I put myself in harm's way, somebody cares and doesn't want me to do it again.

"Because you told me you didn't do anything wrong," Mom says.

I breathe. This is rational. This is okay. "Well, I didn't."

"All right, then. But just so you know, we're going to see the doctor this afternoon."

I freeze. "Which doctor?"

"The therapist I told you about."

Not what I had feared, but only a little bit better. "I thought the appointment was next week."

"I moved it up."

Here it comes. "Do we have to discuss this in front of *her*?" I say. Mrs. Scottie doesn't appear to be paying attention. *Click, clack. Click, clack.*

Mom shrugs. "We don't have any secrets from Mrs. Scottie."

"Evidently." I cut a glance toward her, and I swear she's hiding a smile. "But some things should be discussed in private."

"It's not a discussion."

"I'm not going."

Mom puts out her hands. "I can't," she says. "I can't do this." She looks to Mrs. Scottie for help. "I can't . . . stay up any longer."

She retreats into the hallway.

"I don't need a doctor!"

The only answer is the sound of her bedroom door closing.

CLICK, CLACK. CLICK, CLACK.

It's Mrs. Scottie and me now. Just us, like usual.

"You can go," I tell her. "I don't need a babysitter."

Click, clack. Click, clack. "The light is better over here."

I know for a fact this is untrue. "Just go, okay? Haven't you done enough damage for one day?"

Click, clack. Click, clack. "I don't know what you mean by that, dear."

"You ratted me out!" I fume. "I thought we were friends."

"We are."

"You really know how to show it."

"I can see that you're angry, dear, but—"

"Angry? Why should I be angry? It's not like I'm in any trouble." But I'm so mad, my legs have gone stiff. It's easy to yell at someone who's right in front of you.

"It could've been worse," she says matter-of-factly. "I neglected to tell them you girls had been drinking."

"Gee, thanks for your discretion. Anyway, they guessed." I pause. "Wait, how do you even know that?"

Mrs. Scottie smiles. "It's been a long life, Ellis, dear. I know things."

The knowing smile only sets me off. "Why do you have to butt in where you're not wanted?"

Click, clack. Click, clack.

"Why?" I shout.

Click, clack. Click, clack.

"I hate you," I scream at the top of my lungs. "Do you have any idea how much I hate you?"

Click, clack. Click, clack. "I'm terribly sorry to hear that, dear."

Mrs. Scottie looks up at me. She sighs and reaches deep into her lap until she finds the end of her knitting. The whole mess is shoved aside, and now that she's ready, suddenly I'm wailing in her arms.

16

Rain on a Stained-Glass Window

Beautiful and sad—it always matches the way you're feeling.

THE RAIN SOAKS my hair and skin, but I don't stop walking. After everything that's gone wrong today, I just need to see Dad.

It's not complicated. Really. I don't see why Mom has so much trouble understanding why I come here.

I forgo the bus because I need time to focus. I want to be alone, alone, until I get to Dad.

But there's damage control to be done. I text Colin:

last night was messed up.

I wonder if Abby's gotten to him first. She's grounded, which means her dad has confiscated her phone, but she typically manages to find a way around things like that.

Colin's reply message makes me wish I hadn't bothered reaching out.

so i heard. wtf?

I don't want to get into the details with him over text. Anyway, he'll come down on Abby's side like usual.

idk. she's out of control.

The little green light comes back almost immediately.

i meant wtf is up with u?

I don't even know what to say to that.

f u. f both of u.

I close the phone. When it rings two seconds later, I don't pick up.

I TELL DAD everything. Last night, the party, this morning, the stuff with Mom and the doctor.

"I'm not going, okay? You understand why I'm not going, right?" I reach for his hand. His warm fingers close around mine, but only because I press them into place with my other hand. It feels almost right. It feels good.

I tell him about Cara—he'll remember her from when we were little.

"We hung out for a bit, and it was really good, Dad. I think we're going to be friends again.

"But I fought with Abby. I haven't even told her what Mom said the other day. Isn't that stupid? I mean, I have to tell her, right? Do you think it'll go away this time, like before? Do you think Mom will just leave it alone after a while? She always does, right?"

I rest my head on our clasped hands. "Yeah, that's what she always does."

So why does it feel like this time might be different?

THE TINY CHAPEL separates itself from the hum and thrum of ALF's hallways. The seats on the wooden pews are padded, red and plushy.

The nurses are changing Dad's sheets, so I've stepped out of the way. I don't like to watch the mechanics of their care. The behind-the-scenes, keep-him-alive-and-looking-good technicalities. I don't see him that way.

The rain on the stained-glass window is pretty. I

love summer rain, the kind you can walk in and just be wet, with no ill effects. The ends of my hair are still damp from earlier.

Being in the chapel is nice, and not, because it makes me think harder about the way things are right now. The quiet reminds me that there's no easy answer, even though I've read everything imaginable about end-of-life issues, looking for one. I don't know what's right, or what Dad would want. Except, I can't give up when there's a chance he could wake up. That happens sometimes. There are stories.

I think you're supposed to pray when you're in here, but I never do. I don't know what to say to God or whoever might be listening. I thumb through the worn hymnals and draw on the little prayer request notepads, even though that might be kind of wrong.

We're not religious, but when I think about what'll happen when Dad goes away, I have to wonder. I don't know if I like the idea of an afterlife. It feels like a huge gamble. I mean, it's pretty much fifty-fifty that there's life after death. But on top of that, it's fifty-fifty that life after death is going to be something worth hoping for. You just don't know what you're casting your lot toward. It could be awesome, a euphoric heaven where you never feel worried or hurt. Or it could totally blow, and then you're really stuck. What if heaven/eternity/forever is this horrible trap that's way worse than life as we know it?

Maybe it's better if the end is just the end.

YOU'RE NOT SUPPOSED to use cell phones in the patient rooms or in the hall, but there's no one around and the chapel's all the way at the end of the building. I slide open my phone and click through my contacts until I find her name. One quick press, and it connects and starts ringing.

"Hi," Cara says.

"Hi."

Pause. I didn't plan any further than this.

Music turns down in the background on Cara's end. "What's going on?"

"I don't know."

"You at home?"

I study the stained-glass window, with its slow tears running down. "Sort of."

"What does that mean?"

"Nothing. I don't know why I said that."

"Oh."

"The more we talk, the weirder I get," I say. "You can hang up if you want."

"I don't want."

Pause. My turn. "You got home okay?"

"Sure. Yeah."

"I have new respect for you, after seeing you wrangle all those guys."

"Please. That was nothing. Especially compared to what you had to deal with. Did Abby really stuff her bra with Jell-O?"

I gasp. "How did you know that?"

"Evan was on the phone with Dennis earlier. I overheard. Something about a striptease."

Oh, God. "People know? They're talking about it?"

"I guess."

I should hang up right now. Call Abby and warn her to get some damage control started. My brain flashes forward five minutes: I'll be on the phone with Abby listening to her screech about who knows and how did they find out and why can't she remember. She'll go on and on, and I'll be sitting here, drained and horrified, reliving every awkward minute of the last twenty-four hours.

Whatever force it is that causes me to curl up in a ball on the red-cushioned pew is far beyond my control. A fresh gust of rain rattles the stained-glass window. I raise my eyes to it, washed in a feeling of complete overload.

"Plus, she was just so smashed," Cara says. "Did you get in major trouble?"

I breathe a sigh, relieved to be reminded of Abby's grounding. To call would be a breach of the rules.

"I don't really want to talk about last night," I say.

"What do you want to talk about?"

"You pick." I tuck my knees tighter, press the phone closer to my ear. I have too much on my mind, and I don't want to think about any of it.

"I drew some pictures for you," Cara says.

"For me?" My pulse speeds up.

"Yeah. I'll show them to you."

"What are they of?"

"Different things."

My gaze wanders upward again. "Can you draw a stained-glass window?"

"I can draw anything. Is that what you want?"

"Yeah." I close my eyes. "A pretty one, not a sad one."

"Hmm. They're all kind of sad, aren't they?"

The tears that prick my eyes feel warm. "I have to go now."

I figure she'll say bye and hang up after that, but she comes back with, "Ellis? Are you okay?"

It should be easy to just say yes. Instead I don't say anything.

"You don't have to tell me," Cara says into the quiet I've created.

"It's a lot of stuff," I manage.

"Can I help?" she says.

The pause stretches on for a while.

"I'm going to think about you drawing me a picture," I say.

MY SENSES are heightened. The hair on my neck is up. But strangely, I'm not dialing my cell again.

If I wasn't mad, I'd find a way to call Abby and warn her. If I wasn't mad, I'd spend the rest of the day getting the full scoop out of everyone else who was there last night. But I'm not reaching for my cell.

This is a deep transgression against best friendship.

17
Driving

*For once, for a little while,
everything's up to me.*

I LEAN FORWARD in the chair and rest my cheek on the fresh sheets near Dad's shoulder. They've washed him up, too; I can smell the institutional soap. Everything is clean and familiar, quiet. The machines' steady hum settles over us, Dad speaking to me. I struggle to listen through it, to hear his real voice in my mind, but it doesn't come so often anymore.

I close my eyes. The nurses have dimmed the fluorescent lights for me, and I feel myself drifting. Drifting to a place where I can see him, hear him, know him again.

"Don't tell your mother," Dad says, helping me into the driver's side of the golf cart.

I laugh. I'm nearly thirteen, and already I don't tell Mom any more than I have to. "I won't. This is so cool."

Dad points. "Okay, that's the gas. That's the brake. Make friends with the brake."

I plant both feet on it.

"Good." Dad walks around and hops in the passenger side, where I was sitting a moment ago. My hands grip the thin steering wheel. Yes! I've wanted all my life to drive something, but I've never done it before. Mom won't even take me to the go-carts.

Dad shifts the gear stick from P to D and says, "Now release it slowly."

I move my feet. The cart lurches forward an inch. I slam my feet back down. Dad chuckles. "It's okay. Let go and give it a little gas."

I gun it. We fly several yards before I panic and brake again. Stop, start. Stop, start. Dad talks me through it, and I learn to guide the wheel. He has one hand on my shoulder, the other on the dash. The green lawn stretches wide in front of us, and I drive in big slow circles. I get the hang of it, and soon we're swooping, soaring round and round at top speed, which isn't really very fast, but feels it.

Dad grins. "See? You're a natural."

I'm concentrating hard on my hands and feet, but I

manage to quip, "Hello, I've been telling you that for years."
The world is at my fingertips, Dad is at my side, and it feels
like nothing could ever go wrong.

"ELLIS."

Mom's hand on my shoulder shakes me awake.
She's sitting on the edge of Dad's bed, feet close to
mine, face leaning in.

My head is fuzzed from awkward sleep. It's strange,
seeing Mom here. In my special place, my alone-with-
Dad place.

"What are you doing here?" I shrug out from
under her touch, and she pulls away like I've stung
her. Her other hand is resting on Dad's wrist, almost
like she's feeling his pulse. I know it's beating strong.

"We have an appointment to keep," Mom says.

"I told you I'm not going."

"This is important to me."

I raise my voice. "Not. Going."

Mom takes a deep breath. "I hear you saying that
you would prefer not to go to the doctor today."

"Yeah, I've only said it a hundred times."

"Will you listen to me explain why I want you to go?"

"I already know why." I drag myself out of the chair,
circling around the bed, away from her. "So shrink

number a hundred can try to convince me that you're right about Dad."

"That's not why."

"Yeah? Then why?" I surge forward; my thighs bump the bed frame. On the other side, Mom shifts to keep her balance. We're not that far apart, really, but it feels like what's between us is huge and pushing us outward.

She doesn't stand up to face me. She sits there, hip to hip with Dad, holding his hand, mostly gazing at him, sometimes glancing at me over her angled shoulder. I don't understand why she looks so much smaller than usual.

"I want us to be able to talk about things."

"What?"

"I want you to be able to tell me how you're feeling. And I want to tell you—to tell you how I'm feeling. We don't do that very well, do we?"

I don't know what to say.

"I want to understand why things like last night happen, and what's going on with you."

I choke on a laugh. "You have no idea what happened last night. You didn't even ask me. You don't understand anything."

"But I want to."

I'm not sure that's true. "Well, you can't."

Mom looks at me. "Maybe you won't get anything out of it. I know that's a possibility, Ellis, but it would mean a lot to me if you would just try. Please."

She kisses Dad's forehead, touches him along the edge of his hair. I don't like it buzzed so short, like sandpaper. He used to wear it longer, a little poufy. One of many things that have changed.

Mom stands up, moving toward the door. Despite what she's just said, I don't know what she's thinking. I don't know what she's feeling. But I know that I want to.

I want to tell her . . . I want her to understand . . . what? I cross my arms tight over my chest. For a moment, I wait, searching for the right words, any words at all.

"It won't help," I say.

"Okay."

"I'm not changing my mind."

"I know."

Mom slides her sunglasses on. The keys dangle from her fingers, stretched out to me. "Let's go. You can drive."

18

Dr. K-H

Maybe. A little. I'm not completely sure yet.

AT FIRST, I THINK I've walked into the wrong room. The woman is wearing hemp-looking woven sandals. It's enough to make me want to turn around and leave.

She extends a slim hand. "Margaret Krezinski-Hollingswood. You must be Ellis."

"Brilliant deduction. I'm already cured," I say.

"That's why they pay me the big bucks." She grins, then pats the sides of her thighs. "Well, let's have a seat, shall we?"

The office looks straight out of the seventies. Wood paneled, with shag throw rugs and an honest-to-God hammock strung up between the walls at one corner. All the chairs have skinny arms, except for one fat green sofa, where I sit. The AC's not quite turned up enough.

A black-framed crayon drawing on the wall beside me shows a little green kid labeled "Jeremy" next to a big purple person labeled "Dr. K-H," which makes sense, because hers is about the longest name I've ever heard. That and the plush sofa are the only things that don't quite fit the old-school décor.

"I've never had a hippie shrink," I say.

"I prefer 'retro therapist,'" she says primly, easing into a chair across from me.

Whatever. But I try to sound sincere when I say, "Oh. Sorry."

"That was a joke," she says.

"Oh. Sorry." The sudden silence edges me. "Uh, well, I've never had a shrink who makes jokes before, either."

Dr. K-H laughs. "Really? None of them?"

"What are the odds, right? I've been to like a hundred."

"How many really?"

I have to think. "Maybe six."

"Which one did you like best?"

"None of them."

"That must have been very frustrating for you."

Here we go, with the shrinkiness. "I guess."

"A lot of people have to try on a few therapists

before they find one that fits," she says. "Nothing wrong with that."

I shrug, but look at her face a little harder. So far, this is not so bad. At least she didn't start off by listing what all needs to be fixed about me.

"What made you decide to seek therapy, Ellis?"

I snort. "Uh . . . I didn't. My mom . . ." My voice trails off.

"I see." Dr. K-H nods.

Pause.

"Well," the doctor says, "sitting here isn't going to help anything unless you want to be here."

Silence.

She gets up and goes to the cabinet behind her desk. "We still have an hour, so what'll it be? I've got checkers, backgammon, deck of cards. Candy Land, for the young at heart." She grins.

"Um . . ."

"I'm partial to checkers, myself," she says, extracting the game box. "If you can be swayed."

I sit up straighter. "Um . . . so, that's it?" I'm relieved, but also vaguely disappointed.

The doctor flips open the checkers box. "That's it," she says. "Unless . . ."

Pause.

The long silence draws me in.

Okay, I'll bite. "Unless . . . ?"

"If you found a therapist you liked, would you want to work with him or her?"

I shift in place. I should have known it would be a big unless. "I don't know. Maybe. If it's not stupid. If it helps with . . . you know . . . stuff."

"So, you don't mind if we talk a bit more?"

Pause.

"Checkers are okay, I guess." I like them. Abby doesn't. Which means I haven't played in years.

"Red or black?"

I choose black. I rub the ridges around the edge and pretend I'm rubbing Dad's scritchy-scratchy head.

"Tell me a little about your friends from school," she says.

I scrape the edge of the checker with my fingernail, press into it until the little ridges appear on my thumb and hold their shape.

Dr. K-H studies me closely. "Would you rather talk about something else?"

The soft cushions on her big green couch threaten to swallow me. I don't know how it's possible to be so utterly cozy and agitated at the same time.

"What's the point of this?"

"I'm just trying to get to know you."

"Can we just talk about the thing, so I can go?"

"What thing is that?"

"My mom must have told you why she sent me here."

"What do you think she told me?"

"You've got to be kidding," I say. "I know she preps all the shrinks to deal with me."

Dr. K-H shakes her head. "Right now," she says, "it's not about what your mom says or thinks or does. Just you."

Silence. The pieces are all laid out. It's my move.

I slide a black checker forward. Game on.

She counters, mirroring me. "I think I can help you," she says softly. "If you let me."

"Awesome." I clap my hands. "Let the healing begin."

Dr. K-H smiles. "Do you like movies?" she says.

Uh-oh. Does she know I was quoting *Good Will Hunting* just then?

"Yeah, I guess." If loving movies can be considered liking them, then yes, I like them.

"What's your favorite?"

"*Dan in Real Life*." It slips out before I can help myself. I force a laugh. "Now that you know, are you going to say something shrinky about me?"

She wrinkles her nose. "Wasn't going to. But I suppose I could."

In spite of myself, I'm intrigued. "Okay, let's have it."

"You can tell a lot about a person from the kind of movies they like. Did you know that?"

"Maybe. I guess." I like *Dan in Real Life* because of the family. Big. Happy. Together. Even though sad things have happened to them, they figure out how to go on. Can she see all that?

Silence.

"So, now that you know all my deep, dark secrets, can I go?"

Dr. K-H smiles. "No one will ever know them all, Ellis."

I'm not sure I'm comforted by that.

MOM'S WAITING in the parking lot. She leans against the side of the car, arms crossed, keys dangling from one fist. She's staring into the near distance. No, she's gazing up at a larger-than-life billboard ad of her own face, angled toward the expressway. "Get through the night with WKTZ's own Laura Baldwin," it reads.

I slow my steps; it's something about the way she's standing. I think maybe she's in a mood where she doesn't want to be bothered, or else her thoughts have sent her tumbling far from here and she may not want to come back.

But then she stirs toward me.

"Thank you," she says, clicking the car doors unlocked.

"Yeah, okay," I say, stealing the keys from her hand.

19
Hospital Shows on TV

But not actual hospitals. They don't remind me of each other at all. Is that weird?

IT'S SUNDAY, and there's an *ER* marathon on all day. I stay in my pajamas, pump the AC, and curl up on the couch beneath tons of blankets. They're rerunning episodes from the first couple seasons, so it's stuff I've never seen, which is awesome. I couldn't ask for anything better.

Today, I just want to lose myself in someone else's life and problems. Forget about me.

Six hours in, I've become a hopeless Noah Wyle–George Clooney junkie. I'm feeling a little peckish, but not enough to consider actually getting up for food again. Mom's door is still closed. Perfect.

The doorbell rings. I seriously contemplate ignoring it, because I'll lose my freaking mind if I leave my cocoon and it's just Girl Scouts or Mormons.

But it rings again.

I tug the door open. Colin's standing there, looking strangely formal in pressed khakis and a sleek
sport coat.

I snort. "What are you wearing?"

He tugs at his shirt collar. "My grandparents are
in town. We just came from brunch." He rolls his
eyes.

"What are you doing here?"

"I thought we might hang out." Pause. "I'm worried about you."

"You and the rest of the world." The doorknob
clicks as I release it. I leave the door open for him,
heading for the kitchen.

"Hungry?" I offer, rooting around in the cabinets
and fridge.

Colin settles at the kitchen table. He pats his belly.
"Brunch, remember?"

"Right." I'm fine with that. It means he won't stay
as long, and there'll be all the more for me.

Colin watches with dismay as I slam cinnamon
bread into the toaster, popcorn into the microwave,
leftover wonton soup into a pot, and a box's worth of
pizza bagels into the oven. Pizza bagels are my bad-
mood food. The rest is just for the hell of it.

"Can we talk?"

"I'm not sure." At least I'm not forsaking honesty.

"My phone is ringing like mad. Everyone's buzzing about Grover's."

I slam the oven and turn. "I don't want to talk about Friday night. If that's why you came, you should just go."

Colin holds up his hands. "Sorry. I'm just saying."

"Well, don't." I lean against the counter. My fingers shake. I tuck them under my arms. I duck my head and close my eyes, to ward off the feeling of being overwhelmed.

Instantly, Colin's in front of me, touching me, trying to put his arms around me. I shake and shrug away.

He takes me by the shoulders. "Dude. You are seriously freaking out. Do you know this? Please tell me you know this."

"I know."

"Well, that's something, I guess."

I can't look him in the eye, so I study the numbers counting down on the microwave. The little *pop, pop, pop*s have begun. Buttery deliciousness is a mere minute and forty-two seconds away. Forty-one. Forty.

"I'm kind of in the middle of something, Colin. Did you want anything in particular?"

Sirens echo from the TV in the next room. Colin turns toward the noise. He'll put two and two together and know that I don't want him here right now.

"*ER*?"

"Yeah."

"Cool."

The oven beeps, letting us know it has reached 350 degrees. Colin looks past my shoulder, to where the oven timer is ticking down.

"Pizza bagels and *ER*," he says.

"Yeah." I refuse to look at him, because he knows me. I don't want him to see.

Silence.

Silence, tainted by the muffle of fake doctors faking urgency. Thirty ccs, stat.

There's not a lot of awkwardness between Colin and me, generally. The newness of this feeling makes the first hint of uncomfortable swell to fill the whole room.

"I guess I'll go then," Colin says.

"Okay."

"Well, if you want to talk—"

"I know."

He starts as if to leave, but hesitates. He taps the doorjamb. "Can I say something you're not going to like?"

"Who's stopping you?"

"Just . . . don't hate me for saying it."

"What is it?" My stomach twinges, not from hunger.

Colin sighs. "Maybe you're feeling like this because you know, deep down, that it's time."

He lingers, as if I'm going to dignify that with a response. Then he sighs again and lets himself out the front door.

20

Microwave Popcorn

The sound of it. The smell of it.
The ease of it.

MY FOOD LOOKS glorious on the tray: small bowl of soup, big bowl of popcorn, plate of pizza bagels and cinnamon toast, giant glass of cream soda. It balances nicely on the way back toward the living room.

In the doorway, I freeze. My cozy cocoon place is occupied.

Mom huddles among my carefully arranged blankets, watching George Clooney handsomely saving someone's life. She turns when I emerge from the hall.

"Ellis."

I know this tone of Mom's voice, so I turn back toward my bedroom. Not fast enough.

"Ellis, sit with me, please." She's curled on the couch, a tiny perching bird.

"I have homework."

"Ellis, love."

I will not cry.

"You won't do it," I say. "You promised. Not until
I say."

"Ellis, come talk to me."

"I went to see your shrink," I snap. "Why won't you
leave me alone?"

"I don't want to hurt you," Mom says.

"So don't. It's not that complicated." The tears
are clogging my voice, but I hold them back. I set the
tray on the coffee table and stand with my knees up
against it, arms crossed, glaring.

"Won't you sit with me?" If she could just look less
wounded and pathetic in this moment, it would be a
lot easier on me.

"Leave me alone."

"Would that I could," she says. "But you're stuck
with me."

"You're ruining everything."

She unfolds her legs, leans toward me. "Love, I
wanted this to be *our* decision."

"What decision?" My legs shake, rattling the bal-
anced tray. The dishes clatter. I step back. "There hasn't
been any decision."

Mom wipes a hand underneath one eye. "Ellis."

I'm gone. Turning my back, heading for my room, running from the foregone conclusion. I'll pretend she never said it. Pretend I never heard it.

"It's my fault," she says. It's enough to make me not go.

I'm not turning around. I stare through the arched doorway at the dining-room wall, splattered though it is with framed photos of us. Baby me. Little me. Mom. Dad.

"I shouldn't have tried to hang on as long as I did. I should have let him go, right after the accident. When they first said he probably wouldn't wake up."

I keep my back to her, listening. It's not so easy to hear her say these things that we prefer to leave unsaid.

"I didn't want to believe it," she says. "I hung on to the little shred of a chance, because they said 'probably.'"

I turn. "But you were right. There was a chance. There *is* a chance."

"Sweetie."

I hate the look of pity, the look that says *you don't know what's best*, the look that makes me five years old again. "There *is*. How can you not believe it, after all this time?"

"I'm so sorry." Mom has tears now. In her eyes and on her cheeks. "I gave you this impossible hope and showed you how not to let it go."

I don't understand this. I don't. "What, you think it would be better for me to learn to give up when things get rocky? I don't think that's right."

Mom sighs, rubbing at her cheeks. "I should have been teaching you to tell yourself the truth, even when it's the hardest thing you've ever had to do."

21
Phone Calls

Sometimes they come at
the exact right moment.

I GRAB MY SINGING phone off the coffee table, to avoid looking at Mom a second longer.

It's been a million years since yesterday. So long that I'm shocked to see her name blinking: CARA.

I flip the phone open, turning my back on Mom and stomping into the kitchen, leaving all, including my snackage, behind.

"Hi."

"Hi. How are you?" she says.

Thoughts ajumble. Nothing comes to mind. "Next question."

"Do you want to come over?"

"What?" I say, beyond stupid. "Why?"

"Um—" She pauses, and the whole moment turns reckless. "Never mind, I guess."

"Sure."

"Really? Cool."

Mom walks in, a basket of laundry on her hip and a question in her eyes, still all red around the edges. Chasing me with clean clothes and possibly the intent to spy. It's almost like two minutes ago never happened.

"Can I come now?" I say into the phone. Loudly.

"Bring a bathing suit if you want."

We hang up.

"I'm going to Cara Horton's. She invited me over."

Mom's brows go up. When was the last time I went to anyone's house but Abby's?

"After," she says, plopping the basket on the table by my elbow. An air of April Fresh Downy wafts past me. I stick my face deep into the basket and breathe.

"Those are clean."

I give her a look that says, *What, 'cause I always sniff the dirty clothes hamper?*

"That's disappointing."

Mom rolls her eyes. "Fold," she says.

I WAIT FOR the other shoe to drop.

It doesn't.

Mom putters around the kitchen while I fold the

laundry. She makes coffee and washes the counter-top. She brings back my tray. She lays out the popcorn and cinnamon toast, and every few minutes we stop to munch on them. We stand the triangles of toast on their points and pretend that they are dancing or boxing or thinking about kissing or trying to get by one another politely. We smile.

I fold extra slowly. Maybe she knows it. Maybe she doesn't. She smells things in the fridge for freshness, voting a bunch of stuff off the island.

At one point she takes the sides of my head in her hands and leans her forehead against mine. Her eyes are closed, her breath is low. I wonder what it is that she can't bring herself to say.

"I'm going to Cara's," I remind her, dropping the last of the paired socks in the basket.

"Take your clothes to your bedroom."

I gather my stuff and go, wondering what the hell is happening in our house right now. First we talk, then we don't, but for five fucking minutes there, I didn't feel like the world was ending.

As I'm walking out the front door, Mom's back in the living room, folding blankets and getting ready to bring the rest of my food back into the kitchen.

"Bye, Mom."

She glances up.

"I ate two pizza bagels," she says. "I don't know what you see in those things."

"It's an acquired taste."

She nods. "But why," she muses, "would you want to acquire it?"

I shrug. "I dunno. Can I get back to you?"

She smiles in this very serious, very Mom way. "I wish you would."

22
The Pool

Floating out on the water, it feels like nothing can touch you.

I FEEL OKAY in my swimsuit. It's what you might call a tankini, because it's uncool to not wear a bikini, but I don't like my stomach to stick out. The pattern of red, orange, and cream complements the tan of my skin tone, according to Mom, and vertical stripes are slimming, according to Abby.

I change in Cara's bedroom. She's already wearing her own suit, a sleek racing-style one piece. She looks sporty and comfortable, with nothing bulging out, and I wish I was brave enough to pick a suit that would make Abby roll her eyes when we go to lay out.

Cara flops on the bed and turns her back so I can get naked without an audience. I go fast.

"Okay. I'm ready."

She turns around. I've wrapped a beach towel around my waist. I smooth it now, and smooth the suit over my tummy, and adjust the straps. I'm waiting for her approval, I guess.

Cara looks at my boobs poking over the skimpy bra cups and says, "Wow." I'm not sure if she's talking about my suit or my chest, but either way, I can take the compliment.

"Does it look okay?"

She nods. "Looks great. But it's just us anyway."

"Yeah." I still want to look not fat and not stupid. I want us to be friends again. I'm a little shocked to realize how nervous I am to be here.

Cara rolls off the bed, landing with bare feet in the soft carpet. She releases a sudden swimsuit wedgie with an unapologetic snap, then scoops up a beach towel. She seems so . . . effortless. Like she doesn't care how she looks or what I see. It's her house, though, so I guess she's supposed to be comfortable.

"Sunglasses on," she says, donning hers. They cover her eyes, plus half her forehead and a decent chunk of cheeks.

"I didn't bring any."

"I have extra." She reaches into a drawer and pulls out another giant pair. For me.

CARA'S BACKYARD POOL is perfect turquoise blue. We hover above the water on rafts of neon green and purple, sipping root beer from long straws.

"Where have you been all my life?" I say dreamily. I'm floating on air and sunshine.

"I've been around," she says, and there's an edge to it.

Oops. Not great, not great. I stir the water with my hand, glancing at her beyond the corner of the borrowed shades.

We fall silent. The neighborhood hums around us. A lawnmower several yards down the street. The gurgle of water running into the pool drain. The skitter of squirrels in the trees.

"It sucks, how we drifted apart," I say. "But I guess it happens."

Cara turns her head away. Her raft floats toward the other side of the pool, and she doesn't paddle to stop it. Here we go, drifting apart, again.

"What is it?" I ache anew as the distance swells between us. The friendly blue water suddenly turns too cool. Goose bumps rise on my skin.

I strain my mind, but the summer after eighth grade through the beginning of ninth is a slow-motion blur of still photos: waiting rooms, doctors, Mom crying, Mom crying, Mom crying, until one day she stopped. That was when it started. *Honey, it's time to let go.* But she promised, *promised* it wouldn't happen unless we were both ready. And a little while after that, she stopped saying "if" and started saying "when."

"What?" I repeat. I'm starting to feel like what happened to our friendship might have been my fault. I was distracted, by Dad. By everything that was going on. I was trying so hard to keep him that I didn't much care about keeping anyone else. After the past few days, though, it seems unthinkable that I came out of that summer still close with Abby but not Cara.

"I wanted to stay friends," she whispers. I almost don't hear, but the tiny waves catch her voice, carry it to me.

Oh.

"Did we ditch you?" I say, tackling the awkwardness head on. Screw it. I'm trying a new tack. It's not like things have been going so great for me in the status quo.

Silence.

"Not really you," Cara says. "Well—"

I'm embarrassed. I can't remember what happened. Abby must've decided she was done with Cara and moved on. And I just let it happen. Maybe it's that simple. And why shouldn't it be? Abby calls the shots. That's just how it is.

"Me by extension?" I say.

"Yeah." She seems reluctant to say it.

"We can be honest, right?" Like it's so easy.

"Yeah." More enthusiasm that time.

"I'm sorry."

"Thanks."

She strokes the water until our rafts drift side by side, and we are head to toe. We look at each other from behind the bug-eyed shades and smile.

"I'm sorry," I say again, but the words rise from a deeper level this time. How different might everything be if we had stayed friends? I get a shiver. We both would have slightly different memories, slightly different lives.

"Everything's easy with you," I say.

Cara smiles underneath her shades. "You too," she says, reaching for my hand.

I remember things about our friendship. It was back when I was happy. Sleepovers. Trips to the park. Then I got older, things happened, less happy, and she faded.

Slightly different memories. Slightly different lives. I feel a little jolt. What if the difference it made wasn't slight? One thing changes, everything changes. Isn't that how it goes? We all would have walked different roads. Been in different places at different times.

What if Dad had dropped me off to play at Cara's instead of Abby's on his way to work that day? He gets to work ten minutes later. He walks a different beam, one where the fall is only one story. He breaks his leg. Both legs. He breaks his neck, too, and is paralyzed for life, and we all think it's the end of the world, but everything is relative.

I squeeze Cara's hand tighter. I don't think that. Not really. Maybe nothing so small could have saved Dad. Maybe it was only a matter of time before fate stole him from us, and—just to make matters worse—left us with the cruel task of accepting or rejecting the decree. Except there's no hiding from fate. I know that. *I know that.* I squeeze tighter still.

Cara turns her head lazily on the air mat. Her thumb moves against my skin. "You okay?"

"Just don't let go," I say.

THE AFTERNOON is perfection. We drift back and forth, fingers entwined, until the sky grays over in a matter of minutes and the air brushing over our wet skin turns us cold.

I lift my shades and stare at the green tree tips brushing the pale sky overhead, not hard enough to scratch away the bunching clouds.

"It's gonna rain."

"Yeah."

The air, now muggy and still, promises a summer shower to break the heat of the day. We paddle to the edge and roll from the rafts onto the concrete rim of the pool, trying to avoid a full resubmerge.

We stow the rafts in the pool house, which is really just a tiny shed where the chlorine level is regulated, and run inside.

We retreat to Cara's bedroom. I wave a polite hello to her mother as we blow through the family room. Mrs. Horton smiles at me. "Nice to see you again, Ellis."

A moment later, we're safely ensconced behind Cara's closed door.

"Let's get out of these suits," she says, stripping to the waist. I get an eyeful of small perky breasts and a flat stomach before I turn away to give her privacy.

"Sorry. I'm not very modest," Cara says. "I won't look while you change."

"I have to go to the bathroom anyway," I say, throwing the towel over my arm and grabbing up my clothes in one fist.

"Down the hall." She points, but I remember.

I let myself out and turn down the hall, only to find myself face to face with Evan. He's just stepped from his room into the hallway. He does a kind of multitake, where he sees me, sees my suit, recognizes me, analyzes my overall look, and comes to a conclusion. I see it all pass over his face, because apparently he's as surprised as I am.

Then he smiles, and I want to look over my shoulder because this is the way guys smile at Abby. Never at me.

"Ellis Baldwin," Evan says, "I was just thinking about you." Which is an obvious lie if ever I've heard one.

"Oh, hi." I blush. It never occurred to me that I might run into him here, at his house. Duh.

"Going for a dip?"

"Already dipped."

"Too bad. I would've come down to hang."

"Maybe next time," I say, to be polite. Evan nods like we've just made a plan.

"So . . . ," he says, grinning and leaning his forearm on the wall in a weird way. Is he *flirting* with me?

Cara pokes her head out of her room. "Bug off, jackass." To me: "Is he bothering you?"

"Naw. We're friends," Evan says.

"I have to pee," I say, dodging Evan and the ugly glares the two are shooting each other. I close the bathroom door soundly behind me.

23
Touch

So simple and yet so rare.

EVAN'S NOWHERE to be seen when I come out of the bathroom a few minutes later. I've changed back into my tank top and long shorts, so even if I do see him, I'll be able to handle it better.

I scurry back to Cara's room, let myself in, and close the door. Home base. No tags. I breathe, relieved.

Cara stares at me sullenly from her little desk stool. She uses her toes against the foot rung to turn herself in slow circles. On each pass I get a dark Look. I wonder what I did wrong.

"What?" I say, wanting to peer over my shoulder again, except I know there's nothing behind me but door.

"Are you into my brother?" she says, looking piqued.

"Um . . . no. I don't know." It's nice to be looked at. "I don't think so."

"Is that why you came over? Are you using me?"

I frown. "No. Definitely no."

She relaxes a bit. I feel like maybe it's okay to come a little closer. I sit cross-legged on the carpet and lean against the bed.

"This'll sound stupid, but I actually forgot he might be here."

Cara smiles a bit. "So, you don't want to date him?"

I consider. "No. I mean, no offense, but he can be kind of a jerk. Anyway, I don't like his crowd."

Cara gives me a funny look. "It's kinda your crowd, too."

"Yeah, I know." I tangle my fingers in her dust ruffle, while she turns on the round stool slowly, eyeing me. We leave the rest unsaid.

"LET'S WATCH a movie in here while we eat dinner," Cara says. She has a decently large flat-screen monitor attached to her laptop, and the computer can play DVDs. "You can pick the movie." She shows me her collection, then rattles off the titles we'll find in the family room, in addition to those she's willing to steal from Evan.

"Are you allowed to eat in your room?"

Cara tilts her head, thinking. "I guess so. It's not a rule or anything. Anyway, my mom will probably let me do anything I want while I have someone over."

"Oh." Maybe that's because Cara doesn't have many people over. "Well, I'm glad to be the someone," I say. Mega cheesy. I just want her to know I'm glad to be here instead of . . . pretty much anywhere else I could be.

Cara smiles at me. "Smells like meat loaf," she says. "Okay?"

"Great by me."

"Wait here." She runs away, and I contemplate movie titles. Something upbeat. Something fun.

"OH GOOD," she says. "That's new. I haven't watched it."

Cara drags her monitor onto the dresser and situates it so we can see it if we sit side by side on her bed. We lean against the headboard, pulling the plates onto our laps.

She claps the overhead light off, and there is just enough glow from the windows and the closet and the screen that we can see to eat.

When the food is gone, we lean over and put the

plates on the floor. Cara leans across my lap to do it, resting her arm like a bridge on my thighs. When she pulls back, she doesn't pull back all the way, so her hand is still on my leg. And we're just sitting there, watching the movie with her fingertips touching the fabric of my shorts in a way that's not altogether unpleasant. Casual. Friendly. Like it's okay to be all up in one another's space because we like each other.

After a while like that, she says, "Do you want to lie down?"

"Yeah." I've been leaning against the headboard, and it would be nice to lie down. So we scooch and adjust the pillows. The sides of our legs are pressed together, and Cara takes my hand in hers and holds it on top of her stomach. Our heads are near, on the same large pillow, and every once in a while, when we breathe in at the same time, our shoulders touch.

I almost cry a little, because I never think anyone wants to be this close to me. When I sleep at Abby's, we're in the same bed, but we always make sure to have our own space. The other night when she was drunk, we fell asleep together because she didn't know any better, but I did, and it feels good, having someone beside you.

The credits roll before I know it. The sky is dark,

and I'm going to have to go home soon. I don't want to leave.

Cara rolls toward me, draping her leg over mine. Her cheek hits my bare shoulder. The hand that isn't entwined with mine comes across and rubs my stomach. This time, I actually cry. Small tears that leak out the corners of my eyes because what's happening now is not at all what I thought or what I expected.

"What are you doing?" I whisper.

"I don't know," she says. "It's my first time."

She slides her hand up until it wraps around one of my boobs, which is suddenly at attention. She hooks her finger over the fabric of the shirt, right in my cleavage, and tugs until the strap slides down off my shoulder and my whole boob is exposed. Then she rolls farther, up over me, never meeting my eyes, and grabs my nipple in her mouth and holds it with her tongue.

Oh, God.

Then there's a moment where her knee slips between my legs and her mouth is . . . where it is . . . and our hands are intertwined, and I can feel her shuddering breath.

Then Cara raises her head and looks at me. I don't know what my face says. I don't even know what I want it to say.

"That's what he did to her," she says. "In the movie."

"Why did you do that?" I say. Because I can't say anything else.

She comes up on her knees, right at my side. She licks her lips, and I look away. "What?" she says.

I scramble up, and a little away. "Why did you do that?"

She's confused. She runs her hand through her hair.

"I mean, why did you think it would be okay?"

Silence.

"It's—it's not okay?" She scrambles to the far corner of the bed. "But—you came over," she says. "We held hands."

"And?"

"What was I supposed to think?"

"I don't know," I say slowly. "That we're friends."

Cara's face crumples. She looks devastated. "That's so mean," she says. "Why would you hold my hand, and say I make things better, and say you're my someone? Why would you do that when you know . . ."

I think back over the afternoon. The things I did and said. And how if you look at them how she must have been looking at them . . . "I'm really sorry, Cara." I shake my head. "I didn't know . . . really . . . I mean, you're gay, I guess?"

She stares at me, incredulous. "You didn't *know*?"

"How was I supposed to know?" Suddenly, I realize my boob is still out. I hastily put my shirt back where it's supposed to be.

"She never *told* you?"

"Who?"

She stares. Drops her head in her hands.

"Abby?" I say. "Abby knows?"

"Oh, my God," Cara exclaims, leaping up to pace the room. "I can't believe she never told you. Why do you think you guys stopped hanging out with me?"

"That can't be why." Really, it can't.

"Why? What did she tell you?"

Silence.

After a while, Cara nods. "You never even asked, did you?" She says it like it's just dawning on her what a stupid fucking pawn I am. Like this is new information. "You just went along. You never cared."

"I cared. I care."

"Yeah," she sneers. "All those calls and e-mails really let me know it." She wipes her mouth, like she's wiping me away, and I hate how finished with me she looks.

"I could say the same," I snap. "It's not like it's been the easiest two years for me, either. At least your family is normal and your fucking life is intact."

"Says you."

I roll my eyes. "Looks pretty good from here."

"Well, it would."

I don't know what to say.

Cara storms across the floor and yanks the door open. "Get out of my room."

I do.

She slams the door in my face.

I STAND IN the hall with my hand on Cara's bedroom door. The thing is, I don't want to go. The thing is, I enjoyed myself today. I had more fun with Cara in a couple of hours doing nothing than I've had in forever with Abby doing anything.

The thing is, I liked what Cara did to me with her hands and with her mouth. I wouldn't have stopped her going a little further.

I reach in my pocket.

Thumbs fly over my cell phone keypad.

PLEASE FORGIVE ME.

24
Rash Decisions

Sometimes they turn out for the best.

I RUN DOWN the stairs, making for the front door. Inevitably, I pass through the front hall, which leads past the family room.

Evan rolls off the sofa when he sees me. He pops into the hall.

"Headed out?"

What does it look like? "Yeah," I say. "It's late." I glance back at the stairs, like there's an option there, or like maybe she's coming after me.

"Say, I was wondering," Evan says. He traces a groove in the tile with one bare toe. "Are you going to the graduation dance?"

"I'm a sophomore," I say automatically.

He looks flustered. Embarrassed. Something. "I

know. I meant—if you're not going already"—deep sigh—"do you want to go with me?"

"Oh," I say. I look back at the stairs, but quickly blink away. "Um. Is Cara going?"

Evan scoffs. "With who? She doesn't even *like* anybody."

I say nothing. Cara hates me now anyway. If I do this, it'll be over between us forever; I won't have to worry about what comes next. And it'll get Abby off my back if I agree to a date for Friday.

Sometimes there's an easy fix to everything.

"Yeah, sure," I say, smiling up at Evan. "Sounds like fun."

Evan grins. He is pretty cute, to be honest. I could do worse.

He leans in to hug me, like this will seal the deal. His thick jock arms fold around me. I let my cheek fall against his chest, all firm and muscled. Not a bad feeling, but not what I was hoping for.

Not enough to make me forget.

Not enough to make me sure of anything.

And not enough to touch the thousand stronger sensations already swirling through me.

I pull away. "I have to get home."

"I'll drive you," he offers. "Otherwise you'd have to take the bus, right?"

"Thanks."

Evan slides his feet into a pair of flip-flops, pokes his head into the kitchen to tell his mom he's off.

"Bye, Ellis," Mrs. Horton calls. "Come again soon."

"Bye," I say, and nothing more. I don't have the heart to tell her that I won't be coming back.

Evan swings open the front door and lets me go through first. Then he trots ahead of me to hold open the car door, too. This surprises me a little. Maybe he's a gentleman at heart, despite much evidence to the contrary.

Evan sets the stereo to the local hip-hop station and lowers the windows so we get a nice breeze. He drives fast and smooth. We ride without speaking for quite a while, and I'm glad. The air and the music make me feel far away, like nothing can touch me, and I almost wish that we would never stop moving so that nothing behind us can ever catch up.

"I'm going to State in the fall," he says finally, drumming the steering wheel at a stoplight.

"Yeah?" I think I heard that. "Cool." I wait a beat, turning my face to the window, but the light is still red. Maybe I'm supposed to converse now. Since he's making an effort and stuff. "You excited?"

"Yeah. Should be cool. Come visit me sometime, if you want."

"Sure." Not.

We pull into my driveway.

"Thanks for the ride." I reach for the door handle.

"Hey," he says, laying his hand on my arm. My heart pounds in anticipation. "So, I'll pick you up Friday?"

I breathe. "Yeah. Great. See you then."

He smiles, and I vault out of the car. I hurry up the driveway, feeling very relieved that he didn't try to kiss me.

25
The Last Days of School

I can't wait for it to be over.

IT'S OFFICIALLY the last half week of school, and today is Yearbook Day. The peppy posters are up everywhere, reminding us each to pick up our own glorious copy before the day is out. I groan as I stroll up the sidewalk toward the building.

I don't even want to go inside. I duck around the corner, to the parking lot side of the building, away from the front doors. The rough bricks feel good against my back. Cars pull in and out of the parking lot, dropping people off, while others zoom into parking spaces. A couple of seniors are sneaking a smoke on the side lawn, glancing furtively around like they're spies or something.

I could skip, I guess. All it would take is a few steps to the side, then a few more, until I got across the street to where the public bus stops. It's never more than a fifteen-minute wait. I could be anywhere by the time the homeroom bell rings.

But I don't go, and now my chance is over. Evan's Jeep pulls into the lot; he and Cara hop out. That gets me moving. I edge my way back around the corner, blending into the flock headed for the front doors.

The yearbook tables are right inside the atrium. It's a wash of electric blue—a high wall of spines, with covers to match. A perky blond girl with a high pony-tail checks names off the list. I think she's a cheer-leader. Or if she isn't, she should be. I snatch a copy and give her my name.

She marks me down with a flourish and grins. "Enjoy!"

"Mmm-kay!" I mimic her cheery tone, bouncing my head side to side. Her smile seems genuine, even though I'm mocking her. She's probably nice enough. I smile back.

I deliberately do not look for my picture as I head toward my locker.

ABBY'S LOCKER is across the hall from mine and down a bit. I see her coming out of the corner of my eye, but I spin the dial on my locker and pretend not to notice.

The hall is crowded and not at all quiet. Maybe I'm just attuned to her, because I hear her gasp over and above the noise. I can't help it. I turn in time to see her glancing side to side down the hallway, cheeks quivering like she's about to burst out crying. She gapes into her locker and claps a hand over her mouth.

I move toward her automatically, parting the crowd with my shoulder. From somewhere close by, a guy's voice starts singing, "Shake, shake, shake."

Abby kind of jerks her head toward the sound. The first voice is joined by another. "Shake, shake, shake."

I come up close behind her, close enough to see over her shoulder. Strewn across the bottom of her locker is a mess of Jell-O Jigglers and humongous bras.

Several members of the wrestling team emerge from the gathering crowd.

"Shake, shake, shake. Shake your boobies," they chant. The hallway erupts with laughter as they repeat the chorus.

Abby flees the scene. She charges through the crowd and disappears into the girls' bathroom.

"You fucking assholes!" I shout at them, tearing after her. They laugh uproariously.

At the edge of the crowd, I brush by Colin, craning his neck to get a look at the commotion. "What the hell—" he says.

"Just leave it," I bark at him, racing into the bathroom.

Abby's crouched on the floor beneath the paper towel dispenser, bawling. Not that I blame her. I ease down next to her, and she leans her head on my shoulder. The girls at the sinks just go about their business, applying lip gloss or whatever, occasionally glancing out the corner of their eyes to see who's melting down today.

"Dennis. I can't believe he told everyone," Abby wails. "I hate him."

"Um, maybe he didn't," I say. I have to tell her. I don't know how I thought I could avoid it.

"Of course he did," she sobs. "How else would they all know? It's the wrestlers." She waves her hands, and the tears get worse.

"Yeah, but . . . he wasn't . . . I mean, I think other people saw, too."

"What are you talking about?" She sniffs. I reach up and ratchet down a waterfall of paper towels. She blows her nose.

"Um . . . I heard that, maybe, you might have done a . . . sort of dance."

"What?" Abby exclaims, leaping to her feet. "There's no way I did that."

"Do you remember what happened?"

She paces, silent. "I remember making out in his car," she says. "Oh, God." She covers her face with her hands.

"Sorry," I say.

Her head snaps up. "You knew all along?" she says. "You knew that they knew, and you didn't tell me? You let me come here like nothing happened!" She lurches forward like she's gonna kick me, or hit me or something, but I flinch and jump to my feet, and all she does is pound the paper towel dispenser with the open palm of her hand.

"How could you?" she shrieks.

"Hey, it's not my fault!" Anger bubbles up inside me, from someplace deep. I will not let her put this on me.

"Yes, it is," she says, hands on her hips. "Why weren't you there? You were supposed to keep an eye on me. You should have stopped me."

"That is not my job or my interest. Don't confuse me with Colin."

"I can't believe you let this happen." Abby steams

on. "The wrestlers! I danced in front of *everybody*?" She's screaming now, and it hits me like a punch in the throat. But I get it. She can't handle being at fault, needs to be mad at someone she can yell at. Fine.

I take a deep breath. Somewhere in me is a pool of calm. I let myself sink into it. "I'm sorry this happened to you. But I didn't do anything wrong."

"Yeah, you tell yourself that," she says.

The warning bell rings, marking the end of the fight. At least, this round.

"I have to get to class," I say.

26

Love Itself

*It doesn't look like I thought it would.
But it's going to be interesting.*

WE LEARNED in class that when a nuclear bomb goes off, there's a cloud that forms over the top of every-thing, a giant mushroom of dust and radiation that keeps on poisoning you, as if getting blown up wasn't bad enough to begin with.

Well, we're in it now. The mushroom cloud.

I load up my lunch tray until it's full to overflow-ing. The plan: keep my mouth full as much as possible so I cannot be called upon to comment. On anything.

I take a deep breath and emerge into the fray, headed for our usual table. The whole long length of it is empty except for where Abby sits, arms slack, with her head upon the table. Colin approaches her at breakneck pace, balancing two trays of food. Leave it to him to serve Abby in her hour of need.

Two tables away, Evan waves me over to the wrestlers' table.

I am torn. Abby: best friend or today's pariah? Evan: savior of the hour or he who may try to feel me up?

Compromise: I'll blow by Evan's table and then go try to patch it up with Abby. I shouldn't have walked out on her. Later, when this whole day blows over, she'll forget what we said in the bathroom. It won't matter whose fault she thinks it was. It'll all be past.

"Hey," Evan says as I draw near. "Pull up a chair."

"No, thanks. I gotta check on Abby." Besides, I'm feeling none too kind toward the wrestling team today.

"I figured, but—"

"I don't want to talk right now," I say. "I can't believe what you guys did."

"Wait, it wasn't all of us, okay?" He shakes his head vehemently. "That's what I wanted to tell you. Dennis wants Abby to know he didn't have anything to do with the locker thing. Scott and Todd started it."

"And that's supposed to make her feel better?"

Evan frowns. "Well, yeah. He still wants to take her to the dance. Will you see if she'll go?"

"Whatever."

"C'mon." He puts a hand on my waist, real famil-iar, and gives my side a little squeeze. "We can double."

"Okay, I'll ask her."

After today, Abby owes me big time.

I start to walk away, but turn back. "Hey, Evan, did you happen to tell Cara about us going to the dance?"

He looks puzzled. "No. Why would I?"

"No reason." I smile, strangely and immensely relieved.

I DROP INTO the seat beside Colin, offering a deep sigh to the table.

From the other side of him, Abby lifts her head long enough to say, "Why were you talking to Evan Horton?"

"Um . . . he asked me to the graduation dance."

Colin looks up from behind a mound of deep-dish pizza. "Really?"

"Don't look so surprised," I say, frowning. Though I'm not sure why he shouldn't. It surprises the hell out of me.

"Sorry," he mumbles.

Abby glares up at me. "But . . . he's a wrestler."

"So? He wasn't in on the locker thing."

Abby moans, dropping her head again. Her tray

of pizza looks untouched. Never fear, Colin will take care of that.

"And neither was Dennis, Evan said. I guess he reamed out the other guys pretty good for that. And apparently he wants to know if you'll still go to the dance with him."

"I'm never speaking to Dennis. Ever again," Abby says.

"None of us will," Colin says.

I know what I'm supposed to say. Something along the lines of *solidarity, sister.*

"I don't care about Dennis. He's a jerk. But I already told Evan I would go. Anyway, you're the one who wanted me to find a date in the first place." *And now I'm stuck with it, and I'll be damned if I'm the only one.*

"Yeah, well, that was before. Now we can't go. Obviously."

"So find another date," I say. "It's not like there's a shortage of good-looking senior guys around here."

"But Dennis is the hottest," Abby cries. "And everyone good got matched up this weekend. Only pathetic loser types won't have a date by now."

Colin shovels a slice of pizza into his mouth so fast and for so long that I think he's trying to eat it all in one bite. If he keeps this up, he'll either choke or pass out.

"Oxygen," I say, nudging his shoulder. "The body needs oxygen." He lowers the pizza; I watch his nostrils flare twice before I shove back from the table and stride away.

WHY DID I SAY yes to Evan? *Mistake, mistake. Danger, danger! Steep cliff ahead.*

The thing is, it's going to look to Cara like I lied. Despite whatever weirdness happened between us, I don't want her to hate me. I have to tell her, have to do it now. I have to let her know it was just a mistake, before she hears it from him, or someone else, or sees a picture, or another of the hundred things that could cause the beans to spill.

I find Cara sitting on the same outside stoop where I found her before. Her sketch pad's open on her knees, her pencil skimming back and forth, and her head bent over it like if she leans far enough into her art, she can leave this whole mess of a life behind her.

The sun shines toward her, and in the light she looks kind of glorious. It frames her, makes her glow around the edges. Beautiful, but totally alone.

I stand at the foot of the stairs until she notices me. "Hi."

Long pause.

"I wish we hadn't had a fight," she says, shading her eyes from the sun.

"Me too." And there's nothing I can say about Evan that won't make it worse.

"Yeah."

"I thought we could be friends again," I say.

"I want to be friends," she says quickly. "I'm sorry. Really."

I start to climb the stairs. I think maybe I'm going to sit beside her. I think maybe I'm going to put my arm around her. We'll see what happens next.

"What are you doing talking to *her*?" Abby says from behind me.

I freeze. Half turn.

"I need you right now. And you're out here." She tosses me a look of disgust, which pales in comparison to the one that follows, to Cara.

"I'm thanking her for driving us home on Friday." The lie is out before I even decide to tell it.

Cara's expression slams shut.

Abby kind of flinches at the reminder. "Oh, yeah," she says bitterly. "Well. Thanks."

"Oh, anytime." Cara's voice overflows with sarcasm.

Abby hardens her glare for two seconds, then she dismisses the whole scene with a flick of her eyes, away.

"C'mon, Ellis. Let's go." Abby strikes out across the lawn, so certain I'm going to follow her that she doesn't even look back.

Cara sits frozen, maybe just waiting to see what happens. I don't even realize I've moved until she sighs, and I'm looking up at her from one step lower.

"You'll always choose her, won't you?" Cara murmurs from above.

"I don't know," I say. "Maybe."

A little flame burns in her eyes. "It was fun while it lasted, Ellis."

The slight scratching sound resumes. Her pencil on the page. I back down the steps and start moving away.

"How hard did you try?" I say as my feet hit grass again.

Her pencil pauses. "What?"

"How hard did you try back then? To stay friends with me."

She glares. "Don't try to act like it's my fault."

"Yeah? Well, then don't put it all on me, either. Maybe you didn't try hard enough."

"Maybe I didn't," she says. "But at least I tried."

"Yeah?" I cross my arms, waiting.

"Do you really want to know?"

I nod. Cara lays her pencil on the pad. Her forehead creases, and she opens her mouth as if to say something thoughtful. I wonder how long I can stand here before Abby misses me and comes storming back to retrieve me from Cara's grip. I glance over my shoulder, but there's no sign of her.

When my head comes back around, Cara's expression is utterly changed. She's swallowed whatever she was going to say and replaced it with a bitter, spitting silence.

"What were you going to say?" I whisper. This time I see what I did wrong, but that doesn't make it any better. "I'm listening."

Cara shakes her head. "I used to think you were really strong," she says. "But I don't know anymore."

She picks up her pencil again, and that is the end. Her hair falls like a curtain over her face, and there's nothing I can say to bring an encore.

I can push away what she said. I can put it out of my mind and never think about it.

I could push it away altogether, except for this stinging under my skin and at the corners of my eyes.

I GO BACK to the lunch table inside. There's nothing else to do.

I listen as Abby snarks on the wrestlers. From time to time, she slings mild insults at Colin and me, too. We roll our eyes at each other when it happens, but we let her because it's one of the things that makes her feel better at a time like this—if we are less than she is, and in a lot of ways we are. But not in every way.

I take Colin's hand and squeeze it, because it suddenly occurs to me that maybe he's deeply hurt by what she's saying, like when she calls him pudgy or implies that she's our only friend. Maybe that's true enough for me, in the end, but everyone likes Colin. His misery is mostly self-induced.

He shoots me a pained look across our joined fingers, studies them a while, then slowly pulls free. He wipes his mouth and lays his dirty napkin on his empty tray.

"Here." Abby shoves hers toward him. "Eat another piece of pizza, Colin." She laughs. I hate her for a moment right then, on Colin's behalf. It arcs through me with an almost physical pain, a lightning bolt illuminating everything that's wrong with us.

"God, Abby," I mutter.

Colin smiles sadly at me. He flattens his hands on the table like he's about to stand up. Then apparently changes his mind, shoving the tray back toward her. Hard. Hard enough to startle her into a tiny, surprised leap as pudding sloshes over the edge of the tray and lands on her thumb.

"Hey!"

"Stop it," Colin says.

Abby's stunned into silence by his loud, harsh tone.

"Go with Dennis or don't," he says. "But don't take it out on me." Then he does stand up. I've never been so proud of him, watching him storm away.

I sit up straighter, tuning out Abby, who's licking her thumb clean and musing in a wounded voice, "What's his problem?"

I don't bother to explain it to her. This isn't one I can fix, for either of them. A second lightning bolt arcs through me.

Mrs. Scottie says the people you love best are the ones with the power to hurt you. Abby says mean things all the time, and they just roll off me, even if they're true. The ache I'm feeling now has nothing to do with anything she's said.

That's how I know. For sure.

I was wrong about Cara. I can't push away what she said. I can't push her away, or walk away. I have to find a way to fix it.

27

BE FRIE / ST NDS

Being half of something is lovely . . .
if you know exactly where the other half is.

BY THE TIME I get back to the courtyard, the bell has rung and Cara's nowhere in sight. Just as well, I guess. I don't know what I was going to say to her anyway. What comes to mind is something along the lines of "I'm sorry," but that seems way too simple. It doesn't capture it all, what I'm feeling.

I sink onto her steps and drop my head to my knees. What I want is to tell her how bad I've screwed up, if she can even stand to hear it.

It's me who's wrong.

Now.

Back then.

Always.

I take slow, deep breaths, to calm my racing mind. I remember so much now. Cara makes me remember. She doesn't run from things, even the hard things. She doesn't try to shove them deep and close the door. She doesn't try to cover it with talk of boys and clothes, or booze. She simply lives it.

The memories roll through me like shockwaves. Unbelievable, how much I've put aside, forgotten. I remember how we used to run and play, how we used to laugh. Holding hands, all innocent and small. How good it made me feel. How much I would have missed her these past two years, if I'd let myself.

I remember stuff about Dad, too. I guess because all my memories related to Cara come from before the accident. When Dad was part of everything, not locked in a separate sphere.

"Ow." I land hard on my side, falling off my brand-new two-wheeler for the dozenth time.

"Try again," Dad calls from the top of the driveway. "You almost had it."

I roll to my back and lie with limbs spread-eagled on the concrete, staring up at the sky.

"Get up, kiddo. One more time."

I'm stuck. Frozen. Scrapes on my knees and shins, the pads of my palms sore from catching myself over and over.

My face cools as Dad steps between me and the sun. "Baldwins don't give up."

I look at him through his shadow. "I'm not giving up. I'm thinking."

"Thinking's allowed," *he says.* "But once you know what you want, then you have to get up and do it."

The bell rings, again.

I snap out of the daze, realizing I've skipped my entire fifth-period final exam review. Great. Just what I need.

I drag myself back into the hallway fray. I pass her in the hall as I'm making my way to class.

"Cara."

She sees me and turns her head away, as I'm weaving among people, trying to get to her. The bustling crowd swallows her up.

AFTER SCHOOL I catch Colin at his locker. His eyes are a heavy pink behind his glasses. I've seen this before, and he always calls it allergies, but today I think maybe he's been crying. He gathers books into his backpack, and we share a slow look. I don't know exactly what it means, but it feels as if we've come out on the other side of something.

"I blew it," he says.

"No, you did good."

"She hates me."

"Nah," I say. "You're really not hateable."

After a moment of staring at his shoes, Colin smiles. Cuffs my shoulder.

"Frankly, she'll probably like you more after this."

Colin's smile fades. "Why do girls always like the jerky guys?"

"You're not a jerk."

He sighs. "I know. That's the problem." He sets off down the hall. I follow him around the corner.

Abby's kneeling at her locker, swiping at melted green Jell-O blobs with a fistful of paper towels. From the level of cursing going on, it's clear that she's graduated from embarrassed to offended to fully pissed off.

She sees us approaching. "I need more paper towels," she snaps.

Colin sets down his bag and goes toward the bathrooms. Watching him retreat, I wonder if things can really fold back to normal just like that, like nothing ever happened.

"This is hideous," Abby says, thrusting the garbage bag she's filling into my hands. "Yuck."

Molding the bag's mouth open, I find myself thinking about what it means to really be someone's friend. To hold back her hair while she vomits, to help clean embarrassing Jell-O out of her locker? To forget the mean things she says because you understand why she says them?

I've been there. I've done it.

How about to glue yourself to a car seat and refuse to move because your best friend needs you? I can't think of a more recent example from Abby.

I couldn't even tell her what's happening with Mom, about Dad. I hate the feeling I'm left with, knowing that.

Colin appears on the hallway horizon carrying a stack of fresh towels, moving slow. I realize he's taking his time, instead of rushing headlong to Abby's aid, which tells me things are not the same, after all. Everything has changed.

"When we were in sixth grade," I say, "for my birthday you got us those necklaces. Remember?"

Abby gazes up at me. "Yeah, I remember. BE FRIE."

"ST NDS. Do you still have yours?"

"Of course."

The knot in my stomach relaxes, but only a little. "Here." Kneeling beside Abby, I reach for the wad of paper towels in her hand. "I'll help you."

I have to try everything.

28

Not Knowing

The gap between the happening and
the finding out is so, so sweet.
But you don't know that until after.

I'VE NEVER NEEDED Dad more than I need him now. The nuclear bombs that exploded on me today left bitter fallout, and there's no one else I can tell this story to.

I ride the bus anxiously, glancing up at every stop. *Are we there yet?* My heart is full and pounding, and there's a lot I have to say.

I'll tell him about Abby and the wreck she made of today, thanks to the wrestlers and the Jell-O. I think I'll tell him about Cara, too, because I really don't think we're over, or else why is she still on my mind?

I don't know how much I'll tell him about Mom, though, because I wonder if it hurts him to hear what she's thinking, what she's told me.

"HI," I TOSS, as I slide past the round nurses' area at the center of the ward.

The nurses in the station gaze up at me as one. They smile silently, almost softly, and it makes me trip a step, but I press on. Sometimes I stop and chat with them, but right now I'm intent on getting to Dad.

I hurry down the hall, but things seem out of place—an extra cart in the hall, a couple of orderlies looking large in pale green scrubs. A blank white gurney.

Mom's sitting in the chairs at the end of the hall, across from Dad's room. I draw up short. Has she come to lecture me some more? Or to see if this is really where I still come most days, even though she's told me over and over again that maybe I shouldn't?

"What do you want?" I blurt.

Maybe she's just come to visit.

Mom opens her mouth, but nothing comes out. Then her face shrinks into a hideous crumple, and I want to reach out to be sure she doesn't fall over. But I'm too far away.

"Sweetheart," she says, "Daddy's gone."

29
Carmen

*She always knows what to say
and what not to.*

DASHING FORWARD, I push past Mom and burst into the familiar room. Dad is on the bed, as always, but everything has changed.

The machines have been unplugged and pushed aside.

The sheets that cover him have been stripped away, his wasted legs exposed. Gown tucked neatly. Hands folded, stacked upon his stomach. Laid out for viewing, I can't help but think.

The antiseptic smell, stronger and fresher than usual, assails me. Something has been cleaned. Something of what happened has been wiped away.

Carmen stands near the foot of the bed, unfolding a sheet in her hands. She spreads it over Dad's feet and turns, waiting. Waiting to catch me as I fly in and throw myself toward Dad.

"Oh, baby," she says as I reach out and touch his still skin. I jerk my hand back. Carmen reaches for my shoulder, but I flinch away.

"What happened?" I turn toward Mom, in the doorway, watching, and I realize. I realize what she must have done. "What did you do?" I shout. "How could you? You promised!"

Mom stands exactly still. Her expression is one of perfect, utter shock. "Ellis, no—"

"You just couldn't wait to do it. You killed him!" I scream. I scream at her for long moments, and she just stands there underneath it. I want to run up and hit her, but she is like a wall of stone, and I know it will have no effect. Or maybe I do start toward her, because suddenly Carmen's solid arms lock around my waist, holding me back.

When I'm spent, I sag against the nurse. "You killed him," I murmur.

Mom glances at Carmen, desperate. "Tell her. Please tell her I didn't—"

"It has to be you," Carmen says over my shoulder.

Mom catches my eye. "He had a stroke," she says, tearful. "There was nothing anyone could've done."

I don't believe her. She reads it in my face. She crosses her arms over her chest and retreats from the room.

"Don't lie to me!" My scream follows her, accusing her again of this most horrible thing. But she's lying. She has to be. Because he couldn't just . . . go. He wouldn't.

"She killed him," I whisper, when the door has swung shut with Mom on the other side, escaping down the hallway.

"Do you really think so?" Carmen says, still holding me tight. Lifting one hand, she gathers my hair behind my neck.

Maybe my sudden silence says something. Maybe it says everything.

"How did he die?" Carmen says.

"A stroke," I whisper, feeling the truth of it settle right in the middle of my disbelief.

"You gonna be okay if I let go?" Carmen says, squeezing me before she relaxes her grip.

"Yeah," I say. As big a lie as anything.

"Why don't we give you some time alone with your dad." She pulls the sheet up to Dad's waist, strokes my hair once, then steps into the hallway.

The door closes, and then it's us alone. As usual.

I turn to take another look and feel my heart begin to rot.

That's when I know.

It was never going to be okay to have to say good-bye.

30
Hot Drinks

*There's something about the warmth
sliding down your throat.*

MRS. SCOTTIE BREWS us a lot, a lot of tea. Mom and I sit across from each other at the kitchen table and sip it silently.

The seat that was Dad's seems emptier than ever.

Mrs. Scottie chats about the weather and her canasta ladies while she bustles around, unloading and loading the dishwasher, always keeping the kettle close to a boil on the stove.

We haven't told anyone else yet. I look at Mom and know—in the way that you just know things sometimes—that this is because we're not ready.

For the calls, the flowers, the sudden stream of people in and out of the house.

Or maybe we're afraid. The thing is, we've already had the casseroles. The cards. The banal condolences that you must accept with a nod and a smile. We had it all two years ago, and maybe it doesn't come around again. Not for the very same tragedy, once removed.

To the rest of the world, Dad was as good as dead a long time ago.

ALONE IN MY ROOM, I dial Abby. It goes straight to voice mail. That's strange. I dial her home number instead.

After several rings, Mrs. Duncan answers. "Hi, Ellis. Abby's grounded, remember? No phone privileges."

"Oh, right." I remember. "Um. It's sort of an emergency. If I let you talk to my mom first, can I talk to her after?"

"What's wrong, Ellis?" Mrs. Duncan says. Her familiar voice goes low and soothing, like when one of us scrapes a knee or slams a finger in the door.

"Can I just . . ."

Maybe she hears it in my voice. Maybe it's not that hard to guess, or maybe she's just smart like that.

"Hold on, honey."

I'm holding. Moments pass. I'm holding on damn tight.

Abby breathes into the receiver. "Wow. How'd

you get her to let me on the phone? They're playing this grounded thing hard core this time."

"I told her my dad died."

Abby laughs. "That's brilliant. But a little too obvious. They're going to be mad when they find out—"

"Abby."

"What?"

"Abby." I say her name over again. Much easier than saying IT again.

"Oh, God," she says finally. "He really died? Like, for real?"

"Yeah."

Silence.

"Do you want me to come over?"

"I don't know." But I do know. "No, not right now."

"Oh," she says. "Well, I'm grounded anyway. But in a crisis . . ." her voice trails off. Just then I feel how far away she is, in so many ways.

"I'm really sorry," Abby says, softly. "Um . . . is there something else I can do?"

"You don't have to do anything," I tell her. "Thanks, though."

"Oh," she says.

"I'm just going to call and tell Colin."

"Okay. Well, bye."

"Bye."

The earpiece echoes with silence. I roll over and hit speed dial 2.

"What a day, huh?" he says in lieu of hello. "Thank God we only have one more to go before finals. I can't take much more of this."

Part of me wants to answer him like there's nothing more going on. Just accept a few more minutes of the drama that now seems stupid but took up practically the whole day.

"Yeah, me either."

Colin starts venting about the Abby situation, and I half listen, but half wish today had been a more normal day. Is this what I'll have to remember for the rest of my life, every time I think of Dad dying: Jell-O boobs and the Yearbook Day of Torture?

Colin sighs, ending his rant. "Sorry for going off like that. Today sucked."

"It's okay. Changing the subject, though—"

"Good."

"Because I just have to tell you . . ."

"What?"

"My dad died today."

Silence.

"You decided . . . ?" he pauses, like he knows it can't be true.

"He had a stroke," I say, to save him.

"Oh, my God. I'll come over," he says. I hear him fumbling in his room, before he blurts, "Today totally sucks."

I kinda want to laugh, but I put it away. "Yeah. But you don't have to come now. I think I want to be alone for a while."

"Are you sure?" he says, skeptical.

"Yeah. Will you come over tomorrow?"

"Of course."

"Okay."

We click off. Silence abounds.

My eyes are all blurry. The room pulses around me like a beating heart. I know these walls, and I know this air, but everything is different now. Hard to see. Hard to breathe.

I don't know how much time has passed. The clock on my desk is tilted away from me. I could have been lying here minutes, hours. I can't tell except to say that the light in the room is lower. Somewhere beyond the window the sun is sinking, taking with it all that I have ever known.

This alone feeling is wrecking me. I'm covered in it, from head to toe, and it's pressing me deeper into miserable.

I don't know what else to do.

I fumble for my cell phone. Recent calls: COLIN.

ABBY. I click past them to the one I really want, no matter that I can't explain it.

I text her fast, before I change my mind:

If you were ever my friend. If you care about me at all. Please come over ASAP.

31
Making the Call

No, not making it. Having it answered.

THE DOORBELL RINGS, far in the distance.

I lie motionless, with my face buried in a mound of my bed pillows. The only answer to misery seems to be to cover my face and shut out all the light. As long as I keep one nostril exposed, I figure I won't suffocate.

A soft knock at my bedroom door, then it glides open, whispering across the carpet. I roll onto my back.

My heart lifts. Something I wouldn't have thought possible.

"Your mom's crying in the living room," Cara says, uncertain. She lowers a small purse off her shoulder and hangs it on my doorknob. "She opened the door

fine, but then . . . I mean, all I said was that I was
here to see you—"

"You came," I murmur, suddenly embarrassed for
having summoned her. I smooth my fingers over my
hair.

Cara looks worried, glances back down the hall.
"Do you think she's all right?"

"I don't know," I say. "We're having a really bad
day."

She draws her attention back around. Looks at
me. Really looks at me—my puffy eyes and flyaway
hair, the tangle of sheets where I've tossed restlessly
all evening. "Ellis . . ."

The question hangs in her eyes and in her tone of
voice. I can't gather the right words. They roll over
and over in my mind, reminding me what has happened, but I can't bring myself to speak it.

Cara steps into the room and eases the door shut
behind her. Maybe she senses me trying to escape, if
only in my mind.

"I can't believe you came," is what I say, a moment
later.

She slips off her sandals and toes her way toward
me, kneeling at the side of my mattress. Her voice
comes softly. "Tell me why I'm here."

"He died." I turn my face into the pillows to stifle the return of the overwhelming ache. I tuck my knees in.

"Oh, no." Cara rests her hand on my arm. I shake and cry, and after a while, I hear her whisper, "I don't know what to do," so soft it's almost to herself.

I feel her weight pass over me. She lands in the middle of my bed, leaning over top of me, hugging me with her forehead on my hair. I can't help it—I curl tighter.

I don't care why. I don't care what it means. I just know that if she takes away her arms, I will be nowhere.

32
First Times

When something good begins,
the world is new. No matter what.

I CRY FOR what feels like hours, until I am utterly dry inside. Cara hugs me with warm and gentle strength, so well that I don't understand how I've made it this long without her.

I roll toward her and see that she has tears in her eyes, and she's looking down at me in this *way* that makes me shake a little. She pulls away a bit, like maybe the moment is over and it's time for her to go. I see her face, uncertain, teary. She doesn't know what to do, or why she's here at all.

I've trapped her one arm under me; she tugs it free. She lifts her other arm from my stomach, leaving a spot that tingles. She goes to touch her cheek, maybe to dry it, but I grab her hand.

Cara stares at me, confused.

I don't know what I'm doing, what I'm thinking. What I know is that my head is pounding from the tears. My heart is pounding from her nearness.

I've never cried with anyone before.

I sit up, kind of awkward, and lean against the wall that serves as my headboard. I'm holding the hand I just lifted from Cara's face. I spread out her fingers with mine until our palms press together like we're touching a mirror. But there's nothing in between.

I manage to catch her by surprise, which is only fair, I guess. All I do is lean forward till our lips touch. Just a little. Just enough.

THE DOORBELL RINGS a while later. I'm lying alone on the bed, thinking. Partly about this kissing thing, and wondering why I waited so long to try it. Partly about the girl who slid away from me moments ago, and wondering why I still feel her beside me. Partly about Dad, and how he will never know any of this, and I'll never get to tell him.

The bell rings a second time, and I wonder where Mom is. I climb out of bed and dash through the living room. Mom's door is closed when I pass it in the hall. She would be leaving for work about now, but I'm sure she's not going tonight.

I open the door, and there's Evan. He shuffles from foot to foot, looking less like himself than usual. "Sorry to hear about your dad," he says.

"Thanks." It feels weird that he knows already, but Cara had to call home to explain why she was late.

"Um . . . I'm here to pick up Cara. This is from my mom." He thrusts a large Tupperware package at me. "She says she'll send over a proper meal tomorrow."

"Cara's in the bathroom," I say. "Do you want to come in?"

"Naw. I'll just wait," he says. "Don't want to bother you."

"Oh, okay. Well, thanks." I raise the Tupperware lid briefly. It's full of crackers, cheese, and fruit. "Looks good."

"Is there anything . . . Can I do anything?" he says.

I don't know how to respond to that. I stand there clutching the Tupperware, wondering why I'm not already digging into it. Can't remember the last time I ate. I don't think we had dinner, so I should be hungrier by now. I peek under the lid again.

Evan starts to back down the steps toward the driveway. He clears his throat. "So . . . I guess you're not going to the graduation dance, huh?"

"Oh." I totally forgot about that. "Yeah, no. The funeral and everything is that day. So I can't."

He nods, perhaps a bit relieved. Not like I blame him. The graduation dance is supposed to be a celebration—the best night of the year. Who wants to be arm in arm with Tragic Girl?

"Abby doesn't want to go with Dennis," I say. "Maybe you could take her."

Evan nods again, considering.

"Well, maybe you and I can do something else sometime," he says. His tone is vaguely hopeful, mostly awkward. It's exactly enough to let me know that we're not friends, and he's not really that interested. Not in the hard stuff.

"Sure." Thing is, I remember how he looked at me the last time we stood in this spot. The night of the party, when he first noticed me. He saw a one-night, arms-to-the-sky, fun time at the dance with the girl in the tube top. Maybe even a summer fling with the curvy girl in the tankini. And she's not me. He sees that now. I washed my face, but I can still feel the tear tracks—etchings of the real me, the sad me, in plain view on my cheeks.

"I'll be around until August. I'll give you a call sometime." Evan leans forward and kisses me. Gentle. On the lips.

Nothing surprises me anymore.

"Sure," I repeat, nearly certain that if it's up to him, "sometime" will never happen. And that's okay with me.

So I smile and step back inside. I wonder what he would say if he knew I just made out with his sister.

33

The Truth

Sometimes, I even let myself believe it.

I SCREAM MYSELF out of the dream. The sky is falling. Rushing up around me, flooding me hot and cold. I grip the edge of the mattress, feel for the floor beyond it. My skin stings with pulses of terror.

Mom's there before I know it. She's there, and she's *with* me, in a way I can't describe. A way that's different from usual. The pattern is changed. I struggle to catch my breath, trying to hold myself still.

She hugs me, all awkward, right where I am. My mouth smashes in the crook of her elbow, my ear against her chest. I can hear both our hearts pounding. She strokes my hair. Awkward, but also perfect. So perfect that I can't help my little cries. She holds me tighter.

Mom's talking to me now, but then I realize it's not her talking over my head, it's her voice on the radio, a rerun show. She holds my head against her, and we listen.

I try to remember the last time Mom had me so tight in her arms, but nothing comes to mind.

Dad hugs me. Hugged me. Dad was the one who put out his arms for me to run into. Dad's was the knee where I could perch forever and always come back for more. Mom's different. Mom is the bird you can never quite catch, no matter how much time you spend with your palms out.

"I love you," she says, not on the radio. "I will never let you fall."

WHEN I CAN'T get back to sleep, light tingeing the bedroom windows, Mom pulls me out of bed and takes me to the kitchen.

"I don't know what it is about hot chocolate," she says. "But it always makes me feel better." She brews a pan of it from scratch, warming the milk and melting the chocolate and measuring out spoonfuls of sugar. None of this cocoa powder from a pouch nonsense for us.

I tap my thumbs on the rim of my mug, waiting. Mom watches me like something's about to happen.

"We're going to be okay," she says, out of nowhere.

"You think?"

"You and me," she says, taking my chin between her fingers. "We're going to be okay."

34
Scars

*First they hurt. Then they're interesting
to look at. But given time, they heal.*

I OPEN THE DOOR to find Colin and Abby waiting on
the porch. I asked them to come today, I remember. So
they came.

I step aside, and they enter, but it doesn't feel as
simple as it should.

"Hi," Abby says, uncertain.

"Hi."

She jumps forward and hugs me. I don't know if
this means she does care, or if she just wants me to
forgive her. She leaves her arms around me for a long
time, but it only makes me sadder. We've been friends
for so long, and yet there's no softness here.

"Let's go to my room, okay?" I tug free of her hug.
Colin slings his arm around my shoulders as we walk.

"How you doing?" he says.

"I'm good. Considering." Which I guess is true.

He squeezes, and I'm relieved to finally get the feeling I've been looking for—glad they came.

Abby bounds into my room ahead of us. "So, what do you want to do?" she says, flopping onto the bed.

Colin tosses her a glance that says, "Hush."

Abby throws one back, going, "What?" Then she says it out loud. "What, are we just going to sit here and, like, be sad?"

"Maybe," I answer. "I'm not sure."

"Oh," she says, with a slight pout. "Okay. I didn't know." She begins fingering the shopping bags on the floor. Mom and I went out today for new outfits to wear for all the . . . events this week. It'll only be moments before Abby tears into them, eager to know what I bought.

"Actually, there are some things I need to do," I tell them. "Can we just hang out for now?"

"Yeah, whatever you want," says Colin. "Should I put on some tunes?"

"Okay."

The doorbell rings. My heart leaps. "I'll be right back." I scrub back my hair with quick fingers, trying to smooth it a little.

Cara smiles when I open the door. She's holding

more Tupperware, no doubt from her mom. "Tuna casserole," she says. "There's going to be lots more where this came from. My mom is kind of crazy."

"That's good. We're not into cooking much around here anyway." I place the package on the kitchen counter, then lead Cara toward my room.

Now that everyone's here, I don't know what exactly I'm going to say about why I brought them all together. I just know I need them here, or I'm not sure I'll be able to do what I have to.

Abby's begun to unpack the shopping bags. Behind me, Cara sighs softly as we enter my room and she sees we're not alone.

Abby rises off the bed, limbs spread, like a goose protecting its nest. "What are *you* doing here?" Her tone drips with fresh venom.

Cara stands firm in the doorway. "Ellis called, and I came. You got a problem with that?"

Abby advances. "I told you to leave her alone. Leave *us* alone!"

Cara steps in, too. "Not this time."

"What?" I say.

Cara steams on. "Last time I came here, you shut the door in my face! But that was just you, wasn't it, Abby? Not both of you."

"Whoa," Colin says, backing out of the line of fire.

"What the hell?" He looks to me for help, but I'm utterly confused.

"Go peddle it someplace else," Abby shouts. "We're not buying."

"Why do you have to be like this?" Cara yells back. "Some friend you turned out to be."

"You didn't want to be *friends* with Ellis, though, did you?" Abby's gone spitting hot mad. Her hands shake.

Cara flushes red. Anger? Embarrassment? I can't tell.

"Wait a second," I say.

"It doesn't matter, Ellis. I was protecting you." Abby glances at me. "Anyway, Cara was just leaving." Abby makes a shooing motion with her hands. Colin looks on, stunned.

"No one is going anywhere," I say. "Not until you tell me what the hell is going on."

Abby and Cara stare at each other. Long, slow moments pass in almost silence. We all breathe, agitated. The shopping bags rustle against Abby's feet. Music hums from the speakers, too low to cover anything.

"You lied to me." Cara looks on the verge of tears. "Ellis never hated me. She never even knew I liked her."

"Get out!" Abby cries. "Get out before you ruin everything!"

"Hey," I say, "Abby, it's my house. I invited you both." I'm trying to wrap my mind around what they've been saying.

Mom appears in the doorway, looking mussed and sleepy. "Girls, what's going on here?"

"Mom, we're fine. Just go away."

Colin closes his slack jaw, hops to the rescue. "It's okay, Mrs. Baldwin," he says, taking Mom by the arm and leading her into the hallway. "It's some kind of girl thing. It's going to be fine." He closes the door behind them, and for a moment my heart flies in his direction, because I know Mom is in good hands.

The latch clicks soundly, and it's the three of us. The emotions flying between us are jumbled into a mess. Love and friendship and anger and history. Attraction, confusion. Promises, secrets. Lots of things said and unsaid.

Anger burns hottest; it sucks up all the air in the room.

Cara and Abby light into each other, yelling at the top of their lungs. I hear nothing but noise. I can't hear what I need out of this. I can't find in this a shred of meaning. I can't fix it, and the last thing I need here and now is another thing broken.

They fight, over and above me, around me. I called them here for me, and that's not what this is. I am churning in place. Churning, churning, churning . . .

"Stop it! Both of you!"

They freeze, turn, stare.

I am not the girl who shouts. I am not the girl who shows her anger. I'm the one who lets it all wash over me like nothing matters, when everything, everything does.

They gaze at me, faces flushed and tear-streaked.

"See, you're upsetting her," Abby snaps.

"No," I shout. "You are!"

Abby stares at me with wounded puppy dog eyes. "I just—" she says, at the same time as Cara says, "Ellis—"

I hold up my hands. "Just let it go," I whisper. "Please. I need you."

35
A Good Cry

Today, my heart is broken.
That's how I found the way in.

A CALMING TRUCE settles over the room, despite the fact that we are all mysteriously crying. Well, in my case, it's not such a mystery. I sink into my desk chair. This isn't how it was supposed to go.

"I need you to not hate each other, please," I beg. "Just for today."

Cara lifts the end of her shirt to dry her eyes, revealing her flat, perfect stomach. "I'm sorry," she says. "We're being stupid."

With a trembling smile, she starts across the rug toward me. She slides her fingers into my hair at the side of my face, and hugs my head to her middle. Her shirt dries my tears, too. Then she kneels and wraps her arms around me. I let my head rest on her shoulder.

"I'm sorry," she whispers again.

Abby drops back onto my bed among the shopping bags. She hiccups back tears, watching us get closer while she's sitting alone.

A soft knock comes at the door, and Colin pokes his head in. "It got quiet," he hems. "Can I . . ."

"Yeah, come in," I say, lifting my head. "Thanks for, you know." I wave my hand in the general direction of Mom's room.

He shrugs, making a beeline for Abby's side, noticing her tearful face. He fetches tissues and distributes them to Cara and me before settling beside Abby with the rest of the box. I can't help but smile. Colin, ever dutiful.

Colin bumps the volume on the stereo, and for a while, there's silence except for that. He puts his arms around Abby, who leans into him, probably just long enough to reignite his fantasy. I wonder if she will ever open her eyes and realize that she has someone, in a way that I have never had before.

But I think that's changing. Cara sits on the floor beside me with her bent arm resting on my knees. I don't know what it means, but I can't worry about that now. It'll unfold or not, but later.

"I have to write a speech," I say. "I don't know

what I'm going to put in it. I just . . . I didn't want to be alone."

Cara squeezes my knees. "We'll be here."

Abby sits up, noses into the shopping bags. "Do you know what you're going to wear yet?"

"Come on, Abby," Cara mutters.

Abby frowns. "What? Maybe it would help."

"Sure, maybe," I say. "Why don't you work on that?"

I spin out from under Cara's arm, toward the desk. Abby begins strewing clothes all over the room. Strangely enough, it does help. It makes things feel more normal. Colin deejays for us, flipping from song to song, keeping it fast and upbeat. Cara occupies a corner of the bed, feet on the wall, giving Abby space to work. Her gaze angles upward, perusing my bookshelf upside down.

My laptop is open, waiting. I've got clean sheets of paper, pens, and pencils, in case it's easier to make notes by hand.

We're in a holding pattern.

I've got nothing.

"Colin," I say finally, "we have a bunch of food in the kitchen. People brought stuff over."

"Yeah?" he says, then shrugs. "I could eat. Want me to get some stuff?"

I glance from him to Abby. "Yeah, can you guys get something? There's a lot."

Cara rolls to her side and looks at me, maybe knowing what I've done, maybe wondering why I need us to be alone for a minute.

"Okay," Abby says, stepping back from the row of outfit pairings.

When they've gone, Cara says, "What's wrong?" then immediately makes a face. "I mean—well, you know."

"I have to think of something to say."

"Is there some way I can help?"

I feel that there is, but Colin and Abby will be back any minute. The moment will pass, and I'll be lost against this blank page forever.

Cara drags her fingers through her hair. "Do you want to try saying some stuff to me? Then if it feels true, you can write it down."

"He's the only one I can talk to." I clutch the loose paper.

"Can you talk to him in your heart?"

I stare at the nearest framed photo of Dad. "I don't know. I've never had to do that."

Pause. "Sure you have."

And she's right.

36
Memories

Everything that says to me,
"You were really here."

I HAVE TO EULOGIZE my dad today. I have to stand in front of a room full of people who will never know what it's like to miss him the way I do and try to explain.

As I turn my brain toward this impossibility, I remember a bunch of strange and useless things.

My favorite days when I was little were when we'd go on our adventures. To the park, the zoo, the museum, or even his latest building site, where I got to wear a hard hat.

Ellis, he would say, in a giant bear-hug voice, *what do you like best today?* And I would screw up my face and think as hard as I could. *Butterflies. Marmalade. Lollipops. The sky.*

Aahhh . . . but do you love it? And he would leap toward me, tickling fingers traveling on my tummy.

I love it! I would squeal, struggling through my laughter.

And when he was done being silly, he'd grab me up in his arms and say, *Well aren't you going to ask me?*

Daddy, what do you like best today? But I already knew the answer, because it was always the same:

I like everything, baby. But what I love is YOU.

37
Saying Good-bye

It's a stretch to say I love it. But I think, right now, I'm supposed to stretch.

MY LEGS SHAKE as I walk to the front of the funeral home chapel. The colorful crowd of faces poking up above a sea of dark suits and dresses reminds me of foam caps on ocean waves. What a weird thing to think at a time like this.

I unfold the small paper I've been clutching.

"There's only one thing I want to say," I begin. "It's been two years since my dad's accident." I swallow hard; it sounds like forever, but in some ways it seems like only as many days. "He had just turned thirty-seven the week before. He blew out all the candles in one breath." I pause. "I remember telling him that he was really old."

Soft, sad laughter titters over the room.

"When I was little, Saturdays were our date day.

We'd go to fun places." I shuffle my feet. "He always wanted to know what I liked best."

In the front row, Mom smiles. Remembering, maybe.

"So I made a list. Thirty-seven things I would like him to know that I love. One for every year he was . . . here." I pause. "Really here."

I glance at Mom, who nods.

"I'm not going to read them out loud. It's a little personal," I say. "But just in case he's listening, he'll know what it is I'm putting in here." I step toward the coffin and slide my list right into Dad's folded hands.

Then I wait, because I wonder if it can happen in one instant—to start to feel like things are going to be okay.

I guess not.

I turn to look at Mom, who smiles, her eyes miraculously dry. She gets to her feet and comes toward me. Maybe she sees that I don't know how to walk away. Maybe she knows me after all.

She puts her lightweight arms around me, but it's enough to hold me down. "That was beautiful, honey," she says in my ear. "You said everything."

I release Dad's stiffened fingers, let her hug me.

THE RECEIVING LINE is long, the people in it, boring. It's weird, but we had to make the funeral private and put people on a guest list, because a few of Mom's wacko fans have tried to turn up for things like this in the past.

My people all came. Cara, Colin, Abby, Mrs. Scottie, Carmen. We invited their families, too, so Evan's here, and all the parents. Plus Carmen's husband, who's a beefy little guy, and they look adorable together. I thought about inviting Dr. K-H, too, but I'll be seeing her again tomorrow, so I guess that's good enough.

Mom's list was much bigger. Strange people shake my hand and hug me, particularly some who I wish would just move on. One of Mom's coworkers hugs me so long that I actually yawn over her shoulder.

Behind her in line, Abby snickers. We share a glance that makes me feel like old times. But then the feeling fades.

I shrug free of the woman to greet Abby and her mom. Abby and I stand in front of each other for a minute. Neither of us seems to know what to say. How do you go back to normal after something like this? A fight is just a fight sometimes, and in those times you can shut it away in a room and never look at it again.

Other times it breaks free. Then it is a wide open window that gives you new air to breathe.

But it's not just that. I am changed, and probably she can see it. Without Dad, I'm a new me. A me I don't know yet. And maybe that's too big for who we are.

"The outfit looks good," Abby says, straightening my collar. It's a flowy black skirt and a black and red striped top that she put together for me the other day.

"Thanks. When do you leave?" I ask. Every summer when school lets out Abby's family goes on vacation for a few weeks.

"In the morning," she says quietly, pushing her hair over her shoulder.

The part that goes unsaid says everything. The night before they leave, I always stay over, because it'll be weeks and weeks before we see each other and we have to get a good dose of togetherness before we're pulled apart.

Not this time. Maybe we'll pretend it's because of Dad, or because Abby's technically still grounded, or because we spent the night together just last weekend.

"See you in a few weeks," she says, hugging me. Her hair smells like the shampoo we like, the one we bought two giant cases of on sale at the mall and had to call her mom to come and get us because they were too heavy to carry home on the bus.

My eyes prickle. "Yeah, sure."

Mrs. Duncan squeezes my hand and then she tucks Abby under her arm and they blur into the crowd. I watch until they disappear behind my enormous second cousin. I think about how I took the broken heart necklace with ST NDS off my wall this morning and didn't even cry.

CARA COMES ALONG for the burial, the part in the cemetery where the coffin goes into the actual ground. We don't hold hands, but she links her arm through mine. Besides us, it's mostly family and a few of Mom's old friends.

A quick wind lifts my hair from my neck. I turn my face into the summer breeze and breathe deeply. As if there's something in it meant for me. A whisper, or a thought, or a comfort. The air whips up faster around me, and I can't help but put out my arms and feel it blow.

In the space of a few days, my world's been turned upside down. Everything changed, and it shook me, but it didn't shake me loose. I'm still holding on.

When I open my eyes and look down, the chasm doesn't seem so deep.

Before, I thought the hope was keeping me going, but I guess it was bogging me down. I kept seeing Dad fall and trying to stop it, but that's not what I'm seeing right now. I don't know what to think about an afterlife, but I know he's not falling anymore. He's flying.

So maybe I don't have to hold on so tight. Maybe it's okay to let go a bit. I'm ready to leap. Well, almost ready. If I fall, it won't be that far. The wind will catch me, lift me, safe as Dad's arms.

The next part is easy.

Acknowledgments

Writers work alone, but only some of the time. I greatly appreciate the support I've received from many people in the process of writing this book.

Thank you to my parents and my brother for always believing in me. And to my cousins Katie, Christopher, and Anne for being some of my best book advocates!

Thank you to all the first readers of this manuscript, including my Champagne Sisters: Laurie Calkhoven, Bethany Hegedus, and Josanne LaValley; and the women of my writers' group: Susan Amessé, Diana Childress, Catherine Stine, Vicki Wittenstein, Barbara Ensor, and Holly Kowitt.

Thank you to the faculty, alumni, and students of Vermont College of Fine Arts, who continue to support me and my work, especially Caitlin Baer, Tami Lewis Brown, Rita Williams-Garcia, and Zu Vincent.

Thank you to my sweet and savvy agent, Michelle Humphrey. And to my brilliant editor, Noa Wheeler, for attending to every word in every sentence with thoughtful love and care, along with everyone at Henry Holt who helped bring this book to life.

Finally, since this book is a lot about friendship, thank you to my many friends (named and unnamed), who make life more fun and the hard times easier: Sarah Badavas, Stephanie Nichols Ford, Carmen Goetschius, Shawn Jordan, Kerry Land, Grace Lester, Kristina Leonardi, Eric Murbach, and Bich-Van Pham.

Go Fish!

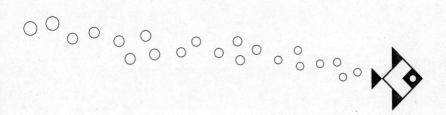

GOFISH

QUESTIONS FOR THE AUTHOR

KEKLA MAGOON

What did you want to be when you grew up?
It changed as I grew up. First I wanted to be a teacher, then a doctor, then a professional ballroom dancer, then a summer camp director, then a health educator.

When did you realize you wanted to be a writer?
Pretty much after I became one! When I graduated from college and moved to New York, I found myself doing a lot of writing for fun, and I loved it so much that I decided to try to make it my job.

What's your most embarrassing childhood memory?
Well, now, that would be far too embarrassing to admit in writing. It may or may not have happened in third grade. It may or may not have involved vomit. There may or may not have been an audience of my entire class. Allegedly.

What's your favorite childhood memory?
My grandpa used to take me to the park, and I would play while he stood around and watched me. He also took me to an ice cream shop nearby, which may or may not be the source of my ongoing ice cream obsession.

As a young person, who did you look up to most?
Probably my grandparents. I spent a fair amount of time with them, and even though they were old, they always seemed so much cooler than my parents.

What was your favorite thing about school?
I didn't really like school, but I liked riding the bus to school. The bus driver played music I liked on the radio, which my parents did not do at home. I didn't know I could get "the bus music" at home just by changing the radio station! It was a real revelation when I finally figured it out.

What were your hobbies as a kid? What are your hobbies now?
Writing was one of my hobbies. I liked making up stories in general, and my brother (who became an actor) would always act them out for me. I loved (and still love) to read, and to watch TV and movies. I'm all about stories!

What was your first job, and what was your "worst" job?
In middle school and high school I babysat for neighborhood families, and my parents' friends' kids. That also might have been my worst job! Twin eight-year-olds once tied me to a swing set. (The fact that this wasn't my most embarrassing moment should tell you something about the scope of the alleged third-grade vomiting incident.) Since then, I've been pretty lucky about landing in jobs that I basically like. The "worst" job I had as an adult, which wasn't really too bad, was a temp gig proofreading legal documents. Very long sentences in very tiny print on extra-large paper. Yuck.

What book is on your nightstand now?
The Vine Basket, by Josanne La Valley. It's about a young girl in

China who hopes to use her skills as a basket weaving artist to save her family farm.

How did you celebrate publishing your first book?
My writers group and I went out to lunch together and toasted with champagne. Then I invited everyone I know to come to a book launch party at a library in my neighborhood. I served snacks and drinks and sold lots of copies of the book!

Where do you write your books?
There's a Starbucks three blocks from my apartment in New York that I consider "my office."

What sparked your imagination for *37 Things I Love (in no particular order)*?
It was based on an idea I had three or four years before I started writing the book. I keep notebooks of ideas, and going back over them one day, I found this list of thirty-seven things I love, with some of the thirty-seven filled in. Many were not filled in, but as I read through them, I got the idea for the character and the whole story started putting itself together in my mind. It only took a couple of months to write after that. Four years, plus three months. That is how creativity works, sometimes!

We won't make you name thirty-seven, but what are five things you love in no particular order?
Ice cream: Preferably two scoops of vanilla in a waffle cone.

Friends and family: Okay, that's two things, but they go together in my mind. There are lots of people who are special to me.

Driving: Ellis and I have this one in common! I love long road trips.

Stargazing: Not celebrities, people. Actual stars in the sky. At night. In the dark, far outside the city. I can pick out a few constellations, but mostly I just like seeing them all scattered and twinkling up there.

My pet turtle: Her name is Tiffany. She's a red-eared slider with a 7-inch shell, who has repeatedly considered starting her own blog about her life in captivity.

What challenges do you face in the writing process, and how do you overcome them?

The writing process is nothing but challenges. That's what makes it fun, but also what makes it so hard to succeed and to publish. First, you have to come up with stories that work. Ideas come from nowhere, all the time, but one isn't enough—you have to find the right combination of concepts to make a good story. I keep many files with notes and ideas on my computer, and in notebooks. You never know when an old idea will spark something new.

Next, you have to make the time to write, and stay committed to it. It's hard, because there is no one telling you that you must write. It is very self-directed. To help inspire myself, I give myself rewards for achieving certain benchmarks, like getting to page 100 in a manuscript, or finishing a first draft.

Another big challenge is that you have to get ready to share your work. The first part of the writing process is very private, and only I know about what is going on. The minute I decide to share the pages with my writers group, or my agent, or an editor, I have to be ready to hear what they think, and to listen to suggestions with an open mind.

Which of your characters is most like you?

All of my characters come from inside me, so I suppose they are all like me in a way. Ella from *Camo Girl* and Ellis from *37 Things I Love* (How did I not notice their names were so similar?) are both most obviously like me. They are biracial, and some of their struggles are similar to mine, like feeling okay about being yourself and finding the right friends.

What makes you laugh out loud?
Funny stuff.

What do you do on a rainy day?
Read or watch TV. I will take a walk or play in the rain if the mood is right, and there is no thunder and lightning. I do love a good thunderstorm, but from the safety of being curled-up beneath a blanket.

What's your idea of fun?
Well, actually, I'm having fun right now. I like quizzes and interviews and questionnaires and surveys and filling out forms. I was the geeky kid in class who looked forward to Scantron tests, where you fill in the tiny bubbles. (Do they still have Scantron?)

What's your favorite song?
Ordinary World, by Duran Duran. (At the risk of dating myself, this was one of my bus songs.)

Who is your favorite fictional character?
Wow, that is a huge question. I'm going to go with Hermione Granger from the Harry Potter series. She's book-smart, brave, and cares about her friends.

What was your favorite book when you were a kid? Do you have a favorite book now?
My favorite book as a kid was *Being of Two Minds* by Pamela F. Service. I love, love, love it. There is no book that has replaced it in my affections since then. My favorite book as an adult is

probably *The Time Traveler's Wife* by Audrey Niffenegger. What I really should say is that I have two classes of favorite books: ones I love for how they affected me the first time (like *Roll of Thunder, Hear My Cry* by Mildred D. Taylor), and ones I love to re-read (like all things *Harry Potter*). But *Being of Two Minds* and *The Time Traveler's Wife* are rare because they fall into both categories!

What's your favorite TV show or movie?
Seriously? You're killing me. I love so many . . . I think my favorite TV series of all time is *The West Wing*. I loved watching it the first time, and I own all the DVDs. I like mysteries like *NCIS*, *Castle*, and *Bones*, and comedies like *How I Met Your Mother*, and *The Big Bang Theory*. I'm not a fan of reality TV, but I make an exception for *Project Runway*.

If you were stranded on a desert island, who would you want for company?
My camp friends, because we have lived in the woods together before, and I know we'd have a rocking good time around the campfire while we waited for the rescue helicopter.

If you could travel anywhere in the world, where would you go and what would you do?
Um, everywhere! I've been everywhere in the U.S., but there's so much of the world I'd love to see: Australia, Japan, Scotland, and Brazil, to name a few places on my list.

If you could travel in time, where would you go and what would you do?
I would go into the future. I've studied the past enough to know that most of it would be less-than-ideal for someone who looks like me. Plus, the world seems so uncertain to me right now; it'd

be nice to get some questions answered about what's going to happen. I'm not usually the kind of reader who flips to the end of the book, but I totally understand the impulse.

What's the best advice you have ever received about writing?

To believe in myself and my voice, and never to let any voices of discouragement get me down. Critique is different from criticism—there will always be people who meaningfully try to help you make your writing better, but it should always be supportive and with an eye toward lifting you up as a writer, not cutting you down. Over time, you learn to tell the difference.

What advice do you wish someone had given you when you were younger?

The best advice in the world is just to be yourself. People told me this all the time. I didn't believe them. I wish I had believed them. I'm not sure it would have made my life easier in the short term or not, but I think it might have helped me attract the right friends sooner. I was very lonely for a long time, because I was trying so hard to fit in.

Do you ever get writer's block? What do you do to get back on track?

Not writer's block exactly. Sometimes I do get stuck on a particular scene or chapter. I don't always know what comes next in a story. So I write scenes out of order to help figure it out. If I feel like writing an angry scene, I jump to that point in the book and work. If I feel like writing a happy scene, I do it. Later I put the pieces together and figure out what is still missing. If you always write in order, you always have to know what is next in order to proceed, but with 200 plus pages to write for each book, I find linear thinking too limiting.

What do you want readers to remember about your books?

My readers remember more about my books than I do! Sometimes I get questions about details I'd forgotten I put in the story. It's really amazing, and so gratifying that my work can have that kind of impact. I would love it if everyone remembers enjoying the read, but beyond that, books are so personal. I'm very content if each reader takes something different away. There's no particular message I want to get across, but I hope readers see something true, or find something to connect with in the pages, whatever it may be. For me as a reader, that kind of resonance with a book makes me feel more alive and less alone.

What would you do if you ever stopped writing?

I might try working in advertising. It always seemed like it might be fun to create magazine and TV ad campaigns. I'd enjoy using my creative energy in a different way.

If you were a superhero, what would your superpower be?

I would like some combination of invincibility and healing powers. The ability to ward off injury and illness, and recover quickly, and help others to do the same. Something that would protect me, but also allow me to help other people.

Do you have any strange or funny habits? Did you when you were a kid?

Of course not. I am perfectly normal. If you ask my mother, she will tell you a grand tale about a little girl who enjoyed talking to an imaginary dog, and who wrote messages in tiny print on the walls in ink. But please remember: I got my penchant for fiction from somewhere.

What do you consider to be your greatest accomplishment?
My books! I'm so pleased and proud and excited that these words I wrote are now out in the world, and being read, enjoyed, and discussed by all kinds of people.

What do you wish you could do better?
Well, I wish I could write better. I'm pretty happy with how my books turn out, but it would be nice if it came easier, or something. Actually, I just wish I was better at talking to people.

What would your readers be most surprised to learn about you?
I practically live in Starbucks, but I'm not supposed to drink coffee. But I like coffee. I can't even have decaf. I know. It hurts. I am forced to imbibe hot apple cider or herbal tea or overpriced bottled water, while surrounded by the aroma of ground coffee beans. I imagine that the tension fuels my writerly angst.

KEKLA MAGOON is a New York City–based author, editor, and speaker. Her recent novels include *Camo Girl* and *The Rock and the River*, which received the Coretta Scott King/John Steptoe Award and an NAACP Image Award nomination. She has also written several nonfiction titles, including *Today the World Is Watching You: The Little Rock Nine and the Fight for School Integration, 1957*. Kekla makes author visits and leads writing workshops for youth and adults around the country. She has a BA in history from Northwestern University and an MFA in writing from Vermont College of Fine Arts. You can visit Kekla on the Web at keklamagoon.com.